I Married Vietnam

[signature]

POW/MIA

Sandie Frazier

I MARRIED
VIETNAM

a novel

George Braziller New York

Published in the United States in 1992
by George Braziller, Inc.
Copyright © 1992 by Sandie Frazier

Library of Congress Cataloging-in-Publication Data:
Frazier, Sandie, 1957–
        I married Vietnam: a novel/by Sandie Frazier.
        p.   cm.
ISBN 0-8076-1288-X: $19.95
        1. Vietnamese Conflict, 1961-1975—Fiction.   I. Title.
PS3556.R364I2   1992
813'.54—dc20   92-11024
                                                      CIP

Manufactured in the United States

First printing

I dedicate this work to my hero.
Living with you has been a novel experience.

This work is dedicated further to the
58,022 individuals whose names are etched on The Wall,
and to the POW/MIA's still over there.
You are not forgotten.

I Married Vietnam

On the day that little Jeremy Freeman was born, God smiled down on him from Heaven and said, "Let me give this here boy a hard life so he'll appreciate Heaven more than most folks do when I call them on home to Glory," and the Devil looked up from the Pit and said, "Let the games begin, the things I did to Job were nothing."

When Jeremy was getting ready to be born, the hot June sun of 1947 was cracking the mustard colored fields in the little pissant county of Connor, Mississippi. The chickens were out back in their coop fussing over the food and pecking each other on the head, the hogs in their sty were rolling around in the mud trying to keep cool, the milking cow was out to pasture grazing and swatting flies with her tail. Vegetables in the garden were reaching up to the sun trying to soak up all the goodness, clouds were floating overhead in the bright blue sky, the woods around the farm were throbbing with activity, the whole earth was alive and pulsating with life. Bees plunged their brown and orange furry bodies into the flowers in the well-kept garden, their buzzing incessant and soothing, while squirrels and other creatures were busy with their summer chores in the woods. The sound of nature was a constant pleasant droning, God's music was an orchestra surpassing the greatest man-made symphony.

The inside of the shanty, where Vera was being attended to by a mid-wife, her own mama, and her two sisters, Lena Mae and Sue, was hot and muggy with the summer's heat.

The curtains made of rough sackcloth and patched in places were still, no breeze ruffled them out of their limpness. The bedroom contained a scratched and dented dresser, a ceramic washbowl and pitcher were the ornaments on its top. An old mirror hung over the dresser, the dark spots of age on its surface reflecting distorted images. An old armed rocking chair stood in one corner of the room, its crescent moon rungs pulled far enough away from the wall to permit rocking. The walls had been washed white, but their splintery underghosts pockmarked through regardless. Although the room was scant in luxury and would never make the cover of "House Beautiful," it was spotlessly clean. In that cleanliness it spoke of pride and dignity.

Since birthing work is women's business, the menfolk were out elsewhere tending to their own like they should. The men were out back in the field seeing to the farm chores away from the bloody ceremony. Although the men were not present during Jeremy's birthing party, they didn't miss the screaming that Vera was doing, or the yelling that her mama was doing right back at her. The neighbors down the way, about thirty miles off, probably heard it too.

"Yeowwww... Mercy... Yeowwww."

"Gal, you best shut your mouth and think 'bout droppin' this here bundle, I 'spect you wasn't screamin' and hollerin' like this when you all was layin' here makin' this young un. You don't shut your big mouth and take this here birthin' like a woman, I'm gonna hit you right square on top of your nappy head with my boot!" Vera's mouth snapped shut and she suddenly found the desire to push the baby out real quick.

The old midwife who had attended to most colored folks in the area for the past twenty years or better was doing her best to urge Vera on, saying, "Push down, gal, push... this here young un is waitin' to be born so push down hard gal and let us see what flavor you'll be gettin'."

A huge contraction hit Vera and she wanted to scream so bad. Sweat was pouring down her face and neck, her night shirt was drenched with it, and her abdomen kept jumping up and down with each contraction.

Inside, the baby was swaddled in warmth and darkness. Each contraction kept pushing him further and further down and toward the birth canal. His hands reached out in the darkness trying to find something to hang onto, the walls were slippery and he couldn't get a hold onto anything. He fought each contraction with all his might, his toenails and fingernails scratching the inside of Vera's womb. Vera lay there in her own sweat, along with her water that had broke a good while back, thrashing as much as her two sisters holding her arms would let her.

Birthing was nothing new to Vera, Lord knows, she had already had two other boys and one little girl before this one. I sure do wonder over the hard time she was having now, the other three seemed like nothing compared to the trouble she was having here.

When I think on it, it seems to me that Jeremy just didn't want to come out and face what the world had in store for him; somehow he must have sensed that someone or something, other than the five women in the room, was taking an interest in him. He seemed to sense that life was going to kick his ass, so he just wanted to stay put where he would be safe and warm for just as long as he could.

It was starting to dusk over, the sun was getting real lazy and getting ready to lay itself down in the west and let the moon do its time. Crickets outside of the shanty were singing their sweet love songs to each other. The men had eaten their supper, which Lena Mae had left the birthing room to fix, they were sitting on the front porch now smoking and passing a bottle between them. The night breeze was picking up a bit, providing them with some relief from the day's heat. Their faces were streaked with sweat and dust from the field, they talked quietly to each other.

With a huge push and gush of blood, the infant's head was forced out into the light of the kerosene-lanterned room. Another push and his shoulders appeared, another and he lay between his mama's thighs. The midwife cut the life cord.

A long, angry wail pierced everyone's eardrums, it was so loud that even the crickets shut up for a while. The bottle the men were passing between them crashed to the floorboards.

Inside the shanty, the midwife had two fat little ankles in her wrinkled hands, she had just smacked his ass like she had so many other little asses a million times before. Never had a baby screamed as loud as this one, he even had a nasty temper back then when he felt he was being crossed. His fists balled up and the expression on his face seemed to be saying, "Don't hit me again! Hit me again and I got something for you!"

The other women in the room were exclaiming to each other that it was a boy, while Mable was busy wiping the sweat off of Vera's face and neck. Vera was so done in that she didn't even have enough strength to meet her newborn right then, so done in that she drifted off to sleep.

The boy's head was something else, the women kept exclaiming about how he had himself a full head of hair. It wasn't nappy at all, it was wavy and still had some birthing blood smearing it. Mable took care of that, as soon as she made sure that Vera was covered up real good, she got an old rag and gently swabbed away the birthing juices. After immersing him in a washtub of warm water and outfitting him with a diaper, she carried him out to meet his father.

The wooden door creaked open and Mable stepped out into the night. She walked over to Sammy and presented the baby to him with a smile. "It's a boy, Sammy, it's a son."

They made a fine picture, the man and the child. Sammy's features, which were usually hard, softened when he looked into his son's face.

"What's his name, Miss Mable?" Sammy could hardly hold back his emotions.

"Vera fell out before I had a chance to ask her, I don't 'spect we'll know till the gal wakes up, 'less you have a mind to be namin' the boy."

All the men looked at Sammy with interest. It wasn't too often that men were afforded the honor of naming their young ones in the Edwards family, the womenfolk usually took care of that right away after giving birth.

Being a Freeman, Sammy wasn't aware of the honor bestowed upon him by his sleeping wife, and the fact that Vera had named the other three never even crossed his mind. When he got a good look at the baby, he realized that this one was different, with red tinted skin and wavy hair on his head.

After studying the infant's face for a while, Sammy said, "Miss Mable, I expect that Jeremy's what I'll call the boy, he kind of looks like a Jeremy to me."

The other men craned their necks to get a good look, while the baby's eyes looked at them with blind indifference.

"Well, Sammy, I best be takin' Jeremy back inside before he catch a chill from this night air. The boy'll be hollerin' and carryin' on right quick, I 'spect he'll be gettin' hungry. I'm gonna have to wake Vera so she can feed him."

Sammy handed Jeremy back and Mable headed inside the shanty to sit with Vera while she fed the child. She told her what her husband had named their son.

The men pulled up another bottle that had been sitting behind one of the chairs on the porch and started celebrating. Each man drank a toast to Jeremy and congratulated Sammy, who never looked or felt more proud.

Jeremy started suckling and Mable sat in the rocking chair in the corner, watching her new grandson sate his appetite. Vera kept petting the long hair on Jeremy's head and feeling the softness of his little cheek. "He really mine?" Vera thought to herself, "He so red, he sure 'nough took after his daddy. My other children took right after me, this one's his daddy's boy, that's for sure."

Mable sat rocking and looking at Vera and Jeremy. She saw the questions running over her daughter's face, but kept silent all the same. "Jeremy'll be just fine with us folks, won't make no difference," she thought.

That's the story of Jeremy's birthday. Nothing really spectacular happened. There were no overt signs from Heaven or Hell that his life was going to be any different from anyone else's, things seemed pretty normal and natural. There was, however, one strike that Jeremy had against him already: the color of his skin. Being part Negro in 1947 down south had its setbacks. All the signs were still up over the water fountains, and Martin Luther King, Jr. hadn't done his magic act yet, so I guess that you could say that things were a bit tough.

The house that Jeremy was born in was really a shack, a shanty shack. No electricity, no running water, and when you wanted to take a shit you had to worry about the bugs in the outhouse biting your ass while you were doing it. The shanty sat right smack on the edge of a white man's farm, Jeremy's daddy was a sharecropper for the white man, tending his fields and making them pay. Sammy got himself a share of the profits from his labor, so it wasn't slavery in the sense of the word as most people understand it. The Emancipation Proclamation of

16

1863 supposedly took care of that. The wages weren't that good, but Sammy loved farming and was proud of his work and he would have done it regardless of any other opportunity that might have been afforded him. He did what most poor colored folks down south did, he worked the land.

Now that you have some idea of where Jeremy came from, I'll be telling you some things about Jeremy's childhood.

Happy birthday, my beloved Jeremy, and many, many more...

$\mathbf{B}$ig jump here, four years, what's there to say about diaper changing, breast sucking and teething? Nothing spectacular that hasn't been said already. Jeremy was a baby, that's all. He learned to walk, talk, and use the toitee just like everybody else. Then Jeremy started moving up in the world and, along with his body growing, his brain began having its own coherent thoughts and remembrances.

His first major memory is about moving in with Grandmama Mable and Grandpa Rory. Vera had her mind set on partying and that was all that she could think about. Being married so young at age thirteen and missing all those good times, she felt as though she had a lot to make up for. All the little ones, Jeremy, his two older brothers Jack and Davie, his big sister Mae and little sister Geri (Vera's newest arrival of two years ago), and Sammy his cousin from Aunt Lena Mae, were all delivered to Grandmama Mable and Grandpa Rory no deposit, no return.

As Vera sat there in Mable's kitchen, her mama let her feelings be known about the situation at hand. Vera's hands picked nervously at the folds in her skirt while she stared down into her lap, her face full of shame. The skin under her right eye had a pulse of its own and kept jumping like there was something alive in there trying to get out.

Mable sat opposite her daughter and lay down the rules governing this new arrangement. "Vera, once you leave them young ones here with me and Cousin Rory, that's all there is to that. Don't you be comin' back here when it fancies you and try to take them little ones from me. You leave them young ones here now, Vera, you done left 'em here for good. No cryin' or carryin' on later will change that fact. I 'spect you best be right sure that this is what you be wantin' to do. I said m'piece, if you want to be goin' now, just be goin'. Just remember what I done tole you."

Cousin Rory, standing in the doorway, covered with sweat and dust, had his two cents to add. After all, he had come in from his field special for this problem that his family was facing. "Vera, Miss Mable done said it all.

You come back here cryin' for them little ones, I'm gonna get my bullwhip on your behind. Miss Mable done spoke the truth, that's all I got to say." He headed out the back door and made his way back to his field.

Vera wasn't too sure all of a sudden about leaving the little ones, but the urge to live some and make up for all of those lost years was overpowering. There was a bit of doubt in her mind then, but the freedom she was after kept calling her louder and louder.

Vera's husband Sammy was dead set against this whole idea from the get-go. He was the kind of man who liked to tend to his farm, sit out on the front porch at night, and have him a taste every now and again down at the general store where the moonshine flowed for a nickel a glass. His main concerns were for his wife, his children, and his farm. Unlike Vera, he didn't feel like life had cheated him out of a damn thing. When you get right down to it, life had been real good to Sammy, until now.

Sammy was one to believe that a mother's children are just that, a mother's children. She was the one who had to make all the decisions about who was going to be caring for them. Sammy sure didn't have the time or the ability; with tending to the farm from sunup to sundown, he just couldn't drop what he was doing every time one of the young ones started hollering because they were hungry, or because they had scraped a knee. He had to work a long day, up with the sun at dawn and quitting after dusk when the moon appeared. He went along with what Vera did, it broke his heart, but he had to go along anyway.

Eleven years ago, Sammy had stole Vera right out of her bedroom, Vera was waiting with her suitcase already packed. Cousin Rory and Mable were lying awake in the bedroom right next door and they both heard the commotion that Sammy was making outside.

"Cousin Rory, you gonna stop 'im? That Freeman boy stealin' Vera."

"No'm," was all he said.

Vera loved the ground that Sammy walked on, but she wanted to head to the big city of Memphis and find out what being young meant. She'd been a mama since she was fourteen years old and never had a chance to be around people her own age who were having a good time. Her love for Sammy was strong and powerful, but those feelings about freedom were stronger now. Her decision made, Vera left her children and her sister's son with Miss Mable and Cousin Rory.

Jeremy had been sitting right there on the floor in the kitchen all the while during the conversation. By the tone of their voices, he sensed that he was going to be staying here for a while, how long he didn't know, but he knew that he would have to get along with Mable and Cousin Rory. Back at home, Jeremy was his daddy's favorite. Sammy would use his razor strap on the others in a minute, but Jeremy seemed to escape it even though he had it coming many times.

Getting to the facts and reasons for this outright favoritism, we come to another aspect of Jeremy that needs bringing up. Jeremy was his daddy's favorite because he got something from his daddy that none of the other young ones got. Sammy was part Cherokee Indian, and that Indian blood was transfused right from Sammy's loins into Jeremy's veins. There's nothing in this world that any Indian brave is prouder of than his son. Jeremy didn't understand the reason for this special treatment then, he just knew that it was special and that was fine by him.

Sitting in Mable's kitchen, Jeremy remembered his father. All the other children were outside exploring, except for baby Geri who was laid out on Mable's and Rory's bed napping. Jeremy decided that the time was ripe, seeing as though he had Mable all to himself; he walked over to her, grabbed her apron hem, looked up at her with those brown eyes of his, smiled sweetly, and said, "Grandmama, can you bake me a cake?"

Mable just about melted! She reached down, patted him right smack on top of his little fluffy head and said, "Why course I can, baby."

After that day, there was nothing in this world that could keep Jeremy out of that kitchen, and as far as Miss Mable was concerned Jeremy just couldn't do anything wrong. As Mable was making her way over to the black cast iron stove, Jeremy grabbed on and followed, holding right on to that apron.

That same apron turned out to be the saving thing for Jeremy time and again. All the times that Jeremy had done something wrong, Mable would protect him from Cousin Rory's whippings. She would wrap Jeremy right up inside the apron, hold him real tight. "Cousin Rory, my baby didn't do no wrong. Was them older chillen that made 'im go into that chicken coop and take them birds, told 'im that if he didn't bring 'em down yonder by the river in that sack," she'd point, "that they'd tear 'im up. The older chillen had that hot grease goin' and commenced to cookin' them birds. The older chillen's to blame, not my baby."

That first day, Mable got her big ceramic bowl off the shelf above the stove where supper was simmering over the wood-burning fire and set it down on the table where Jeremy was sitting in a chair watching Mable's every move.

There was an old kerosene lantern in the middle of the rough wooden table, the sackcloth curtains kept sucking lazily in and out of the open kitchen window when the summer breeze caught them. Jeremy looked around him and decided that he was surely going to like it here.

Soon the smell of baking cake wafted outside of the shanty and into the bedroom. A sleepy-eyed Geri joined her brother in the kitchen, and they shared the bowl that had the remaining cake batter clinging to the sides.

Mable looked over at her two grandchildren and felt

young again, it had been a long, long while since little ones had graced her kitchen. She was worried about Vera and Sammy, but she figured that once the girl got the nonsense out of her head things would settle back down to normal.

If Vera wanted these babies back then, well that was just too bad. Mable had meant what she had said. She would give up the three oldest to their mama, but she meant what she had said when saying Jeremy and Geri wouldn't be going anywhere. When the time came, the children themselves refused to leave grandmama. Miss Mable became their mama in spirit and in every other sense that they could see, there was nothing in the world that would ever change that.

It was a no deposit, no return situation from the bottom of their hearts.

About that apron hugging, I am not trying to imply that Jeremy did the things he did out of meanness or for any other low-down reason. He did what he did because he was doing what any child who had a natural or gained advantage over others would do. I know for a fact that he wasn't exploiting Miss Mable, or his daddy for that matter. He loved Miss Mable and still loves Miss Mable more than he can say.

When Jeremy started growing up and started getting himself some formal education, he would sit with Mable for hours at a time and read to her from the Good Book. Mable would be sitting there in her kitchen hand sewing swatches of rags together, and Jeremy would be sitting there on the floor reading to her from the Books of Psalms, Ruth, Matthew, Mark, Luke… practically the entire Book over the course of the years. He would also sit there with her while he was doing his school lessons and would read to her from the papers he wrote.

"Baby, that don't sound quite right. I 'spect that folks that know 'bout all them things you writin' 'bout would understand. I don't quite follow you son, mayhap you best write a speck more 'bout it."

This way Jeremy learned how to express himself fully and completely and how to put his all into whatever he was doing.

As time went by the bond between Mable and Jeremy grew even stronger. Mable would be out in her vegetable garden weeding under the hot summer sun, and Jeremy would pop right up behind her with a big topaz-colored sunflower in his hand that he had spent the entire morning looking for and, after finding the perfect one, picking all of the bugs out.

When Jeremy first started going to school, his intelligence was noticed right away by the school teacher. I know you all have seen "Little House on the Prairie," well, Jeremy's school looked almost like that, except that it was much shabbier than the little television schoolhouse. All the children were crammed into one room and, unlike "Little House," all the children were black. All black except for Jeremy.

Children are known to be real mean to each other some times, and Jeremy's differences were soon used against him. The other children in the school started calling Jeremy "half-breed" and, needless to say, Jeremy didn't like it all that much. He started proving himself in the best way he knew, he started working harder and harder on his lessons. He'd try harder just to show the others that he was better than those verbal stones they were chucking at him and he soon became the teacher's pet. This just made matters worse.

It soon became clear to the boys in his class that the girls didn't give two hoots about Jeremy's being a "half-breed," they thought that Jeremy was right cute and right smart too. His kinky-haired rivals found this reason enough to start hurling more than verbal abuse at Jeremy, they started chucking missiles now, both fists and stones.

Jeremy's popularity with the girls and with authority figures, his red complexion, his wits and quick intelligence, and the silent treatment that he gave to most folks, all added up to the fact that Jeremy became a loner, and it taught him how to fight.

When Jeremy would get home from school, on the days that he was particularly upset from all the haranguing he took, he would go out back and find a tree in the woods that looked like it was fit for his purposes. After chopping the tree down his brother Davie would help so far as the two-man sawing went. As soon as Jeremy would get all those rounds piled up out back, he would start splitting. You could tell by the amount of wood that he split just how upset he was.

Miss Mable sure did appreciate having all of this cooking wood ready to throw into the stove and not having to ask the young ones to go out and fetch her some. That is another thing that endeared Jeremy to Miss Mable, although I don't believe that he knew that Mable thought that he was doing it for her. When Jeremy saw red he had to do something, or he just might wind up hurting somebody. All that good exercise developed his chest and shoulders into a fine figure.

Jeremy was just nine, sitting there in the one room schoolhouse listening to what the teacher was saying. She was trying to explain to her class exactly what causes rainbows. She was saying how the light refraction from the moisture in the air during a sun shower caused all the colors to appear in an arc in the sky. All of the children were a bit antsy, it was getting pretty close to lunch time, so they sat there squirming in their seats and hoping that the teacher would stop blabbing real quick.

Miss Francis saw that the children were getting restless so she decided to make things interesting by telling how there is a pot of gold at the end of each and every rainbow. That caught their attention, perking them up a bit, and they asked her how she knew. She told them about the old legend of leprechauns, and she enjoyed seeing the sparkle in their eyes.

Lunch time finally rolled around after many questions about the pot of gold and Jeremy grabbed the bag that Miss Mable had packed for him and headed out back to the playground behind the schoolhouse. He found a real secluded corner, far away from the other children, and sat there by himself thinking about what his teacher had said. The other children's screams and laughter were unheard by Jeremy, he just sat there by himself dreaming.

Later on that very week there just had to be a sun shower. He was out back in the late afternoon messing with Bess and Clara, the two mules in the pasture, when the rain started coming down in a soft drizzle. The beads were glistening in the sunlight and looked like diamonds falling down from Heaven. He turned his face up toward the sky and opened his mouth to catch the rain's sweetness. There it was, the multicolored arc of cherry, mandarin, lemon, lime, and sapphire pointing to the south where the woods grew their thickest.

Jeremy took off running as fast as he could, plowing through the woods trying to find a clearing so he could see the rainbow in the sky. The rain started coming down harder, and the water hitting the leaves on the trees sounded like a million tiny hands clapping together, encouraging Jeremy to run harder and faster. Jeremy kept going, not feeling the branches ripping his flesh or the spiny burrs scraping his lower legs. The only thing that he was thinking about was getting to that pot of gold for Miss Mable. Jeremy kept traveling south hoping to get to that pot of gold before anyone else did. He ran until he couldn't run anymore. Exhaustion overcame him, and Jeremy stretched out to rest for just a little while.

Hunger woke Jeremy rather than the sound of nature around him. He lay there curled in a little ball, his feet caked with mud and specks of dirt hanging in his hair. Jeremy rubbed his eyes, he remembered the rainbow, and scanned the sky hoping it would still be there.

Gone. Jeremy's heart sank. He lay there for a while ignoring his hunger pangs as best he could, a sense of despair growing in him. He searched his brain for another way to fulfill his dreams. His mind is raced a hundred miles a minute, conjecturing, rejecting, and then tears came and overpowered him with hopelessness and grief. Lord knows how many tears later, Jeremy absent-mindedly wiped the snot away from under his nose with his arm and checked the sky once more. No rainbow. He bit his tongue to stop a fresh onrush of tears, then noticed for the first time all the scratches and cuts on his body. After looking himself over, he shrugged the cuts and bruises off; they didn't hurt as much as that rainbow being gone, anyway. Jeremy got to his feet and set out to find his way back home.

Cousin Rory and the men on the nearby farms had been out through most of the night looking for Jeremy, and after breakfast Rory went out again. About noon-time, Cousin Rory returned to the farm to tell Mable that there still was no sign of the boy. The noon meal was eaten in silence, all the children sat glumly around the table, Jeremy's place noticeably empty. Mable kept glancing out of the window, unable to eat a thing on her plate.

When Rory finished eating he went out to begin his day's work, with the thought in mind that after he did the very necessary things he would head back to the woods in yet another direction.

The back door of the shanty opened, and in walked a tired, dejected, and bruised little boy. Mable turned around expecting to see Rory standing there, saw who it was, and ran to him. The other children heard the commotion and came running out from their rooms.

"Davie, go fetch Mr. Rory, tell 'im the boy done came home," Miss Mable said, and then to Jeremy, "Baby, why you scare us all so powerful bad? Where you been, baby?"

Jeremy told the story about the pot of gold and Mable listened with amazement. Jack and Sammy both had to hide snickers behind their hands, Mae did the same.

Cousin Rory and Davie came rushing in, "I want you all young ones to go to your rooms, 'cept Jeremy," Rory said.

Mable told the story to Rory. After hearing what Mable had to say, Cousin Rory decided that the barn wouldn't be proper on this occasion, there were no lessons to be learned so a whipping wasn't right. He didn't think that the boy would be chasing rainbows again any day soon.

One evening in the spring of the year Jeremy turned fourteen, Rory gathered the family into Mable's kitchen. He had an announcement to make: they were moving to a farm of their own. No more sharecropping, this would be Independence Day for sure! They were moving to the big town of Renault, Mississippi.

A month after they had settled into the new house, July had rolled around and Davie got to missing his brother and told Vera that he had a mind to go and visit. She agreed and scratched up enough cash for Davie to take the train to Renault from Memphis.

Sammy and Vera were never able to reconcile their differences, and finally Sammy left Mississippi altogether and headed down to Florida. He had always wanted to see the ocean. Jeremy, being old enough now to understand what had happened, began to resent Vera. He was his daddy's boy, that's for sure. For work, Jeremy would join Cousin Rory in the field, picking away at the cotton, while Geri was learning about housekeeping, cooking, gardening and such from Miss Mable. For Jeremy, picking cotton didn't seem so bad anymore, knowing that his family could keep the money they made from it.

Although Jeremy spent the majority of his time during this particular summer at the farm, there were times when he went exploring all by himself. There was a fine set of woods around this home too, and Jeremy soon found himself a place that he thought of as being all his own. He went to this secret place whenever he wanted to dream about the future and he made sure that nobody else knew about it. It was way up on top of a very densely wooded hill, where Jeremy could look down onto the farm and see what was going on. He could see Cousin Rory and Davie down in the field and see Geri weeding Miss Mable's garden. He could see all the neighboring farms and the activity there too. He liked this place, he felt like he was looking down on the rest of the world, the farms looked like little maps from this vantage point.

Jeremy would spend his hours there thinking about many things, but the thing that most occupied his mind was the upcoming school year. He had heard many stories about how young men could make their way by playing football, and dreamt about his own success. Many young men had gotten scholarships to universities by their skill on the football field, and this thought took on the form of another rainbow.

Jeremy felt, that summer, that he had everything to be grateful for and everything to live for. These thoughts were reflected in his eyes and his smile, which never failed to charm young girls. He loved to dream about the future, and he stayed away from the farm to nurture these thoughts.

Jeremy's secret place was a sanctuary now. No one to this day knows where Jeremy's secret place is, and no one ever will. If someone happened to wander along its path, I'm sure that the spirit of Jeremy's youth that was fostered there and that died there would frighten them away.

The morning of the first day of school finally arrived. It had been the longest summer that Jeremy could remember. Those weren't butterflies in his stomach, they were huge bumblebees stinging the walls of his insides. Jeremy got his best pair of blue jeans out of the closet, along with the little white short-sleeved shirt that he always wore when he went to church with Miss Mable on Sundays. His blue jeans had patches on both knees and one on the ass where they had worn through by the back pocket. A little red bow tie was the final touch.

Jeremy was too excited to eat the breakfast this morning that Miss Mable had prepared for him. He felt like someone had actually dashed him with cold water.

After much fussing by Miss Mable to make sure that his bow tie was straight, Jeremy finally escaped out of the back door and made his way around to the front to go down the dirt road in the direction of Cora Puttman High.

Jeremy had passed the outside of the school many times before, so it wasn't a shock to him when he saw the great size of the structure close up. When he walked inside, however, and saw all the corridors leading in different directions, he didn't quite know what to make of it. It was nothing like the one-room schoolhouse he had been used to for the past eight years.

Despite all of Jeremy's nervousness, he noticed that hanging on the wall, directly in front of the doors that he had just entered, there was a bulletin board with long lists. He walked closer up to them and saw that it was an alphabetical roster of all those attending Cora Puttman High. He looked until he found his name, and scanned across to where the little dots led to his homeroom number, which was 203. Now all he had to do was figure out which one of the corridors would take him to the 200 wing of the building. He didn't want to ask anybody, I guess that you could say that Jeremy was just a little bit shy. He decided to go for it by himself and figured that if he didn't run into the 200 numbers in one corridor, that he could always backtrack and try another one.

As he was standing there trying to make up his mind, he heard laughter and giggling. Jeremy looked around him and saw the promise; there were girls, acres and acres of girls. There were tall ones, short ones, fat ones, thin ones, dark ones, pretty ones, light ones, ugly ones, girls, girls, girls. He couldn't believe his eyes.

I don't know if it was luck or if he had a guardian angel guiding him, but the first corridor that Jeremy turned into was the right one. The odd numbered rooms were on the left, and the even numbered rooms were on the right. As he started walking he saw to his right that the first room was 200, the next room he encountered to the left was 201.

Walking down the corridor, Jeremy noticed the way most of the other boys were dressed; he didn't see any patches on most others' jeans and started feeling very uncomfortable. He decided right away that he would have to get some work after school to rectify this situation. Most of the other boys were wearing Banlon shirts with socks that matched, and brown loafers.

The double doors to room 203 were open, and they looked like the jaws of some huge creature that wanted to eat him up and swallow him. There were students already sitting in the room and when Jeremy walked through the door he didn't know where he should sit down. He didn't realize that all of the occupants of the room were freshmen too, and that they were just as nervous as he was. He finally decided that he would sit in a desk in the back row until he could get himself accustomed, and to keep an eye on what was going on around and in front of him.

When the teacher walked in, the class acted like someone had put a muzzle on their mouths. Silence greeted her. She wrote her name, Mrs. Callahan, on the blackboard and picked up her clipboard to commence calling out names. Then the students had to get up and tell the class briefly about themselves. This was done in alphabetical order, and when they started getting around to the Fs, Jeremy began to feel nervous. There were writhing snakes in his stomach now, too. When his turn came around he stood up and stated that he was new to Renault and that he was originally from Connor, Mississippi. He said that he liked hunting and fishing and that he wanted to play football. When Jeremy finally sat down, there was sweat running down his face and neck.

Now that all the students had stood up and introduced themselves, the teacher passed out the class assignments. Jeremy had to walk all the way up that aisle to the desk to grab his class assignments, and he noticed the way that some of the boys were sneering at his clothes. He decided that he had to change the situation just as soon as he possibly could.

There were different faces in each class that Jeremy went to that day, but he did see a couple of familiar ones from his homeroom. Books were passed out in math, social studies, science, and English, and each teacher outlined what the first semester's study would cover.

By the time 3:00 finally arrived and the dismissal bell rang, Jeremy was about fed up with all of the introductory nonsense and was anxious to get into the real meat of the studies. His gym class, which came right before lunch, was the most exciting thing to him that entire day. The coach had talked about all the different sports, and told the young men that their aptitudes would be tested over the course of the next few weeks. Jeremy hadn't played much football, little to none as a matter of fact, but he knew that he could run, he knew that he was strong, and he knew that if he put his mind into anything that he could do it.

Jeremy's freshman year turned out to be just as successful as he knew it would be. After a week or two, he lost most of his shyness and he started to delve into his studies like he had during his time in the little schoolhouse. When the first semester grades came out, Jeremy made the Dean's List, he earned all A's, and he was on the freshman football team.

Jeremy quickly found himself odd jobs after school. For a time on weekends, he sold sandwiches on the train line from Renault to Memphis and back. He worked for the owner of the little café in the Renault train station, who paid him $5 a week for hawking egg salad, chicken salad, and bologna and cheese sandwiches for thirty-five cents apiece. These jobs, and a few others, were finally putting money in Jeremy's pockets.

The first thing Jeremy did was to spruce up his wardrobe. When he wore a red Banlon shirt, he wore little red socks to match, and he got those nice brown loafers just like everybody else. His jeans were brand new Levis, now without patches. Soon Banlon shirts in all the colors of the rainbow hung in Jeremy's closet. Jeremy had to change just one more thing to fit in at high school: all of the other boys had their hair cropped short. Jeremy had Miss Mable cut his hair in the same manner. By the time the freshman year was over, Jeremy had made the Dean's List again. Miss Mable and Cousin Rory were real proud of him.

Jeremy's sophomore year started out in the same fashion, except that the nervousness wasn't there like it was during his first year. He had met a girl named Sara, and he thought that she was the prettiest girl in the whole high school, so did all the other boys. Sara and Jeremy were an item, however, and it was well known by all that Sara was Jeremy's girl. Everyone expected them to marry after graduation. As Sara was on the Dean's List too, it seemed to be a perfect match. They were both popular with everyone.

Jeremy was feeling like his dreams and life were going just as he had planned. He spent the summer after his sophomore year helping out around the farm and maintaining his jobs in town, anxious for his junior year to begin.

43

By the time the second semester was over in Jeremy's junior year of high school, his football coach had sat him down and had told him that there were many opportunities and that Jeremy had the talents to open up the doors. College scouts usually dropped by periodically to check out some of the new talent with college scholarships in mind.

Those words sounded wonderful to Jeremy. He would spend hours with his sister Geri, who had started her freshman year, and they would plan what Jeremy would do for the family once he joined a professional football team after college. They both realized that there was great money to be made this way, and there was no way that anyone could have dissuaded Jeremy from counting on this.

One afternoon, as he was sitting in his world history class, he got a note to come and see his coach in the gym right away. Jeremy was shaking with excitement and anticipation as he walked down the corridor. His feet kept wanting to move faster, but he forced himself not to run.

When he reached the door to his coach's office, he knocked and coach Davis said, "Come on in, Jeremy."

There was a man sitting there with the coach whom Jeremy didn't recognize.

"Jeremy, this is Mr. Howard Walker."

Jeremy and Mr. Walker shook hands.

Howard talked, and Jeremy listened, about the prospects of Jeremy attending college at Jackson State University in Mississippi. Jeremy knew that the pot of gold would be his this time for sure, and he couldn't wait to get home and tell the family. Jeremy didn't walk home that day, he floated on a cloud. The entire family was awestruck. No one in the Edwards family, or the Freeman family for that matter, had ever even graduated high school. The thought that Jeremy would soon be going to Jackson State University on a scholarship he had earned was a real source of pride.

Jeremy, after sharing the news, took off to his secret place to let all this soak in. He couldn't believe it.

It was the last football game of the regular season of Jeremy's junior year. It happened in the third quarter, third down and seven to go with the score tied 21–21. The Cora Puttman quarterback called the play in the huddle where he would hand off to Jeremy, the running back, on three. Offense and defense lined up on the forty-yard line.

"Hut, hut, hut... "

Jeremy took the ball and ran toward the sideline where he knew he would have a good chance of cutting up the field to get the first down. A 200-pound defensive tackle on the visiting team had another idea, he had read the play perfectly. He hit Jeremy with everything he had, and when he landed on top of Jeremy he heard the loud crack that Jeremy's shinbone made as it snapped.

The leg was set in the emergency room of the Memphis hospital, and after the wound was sutured up and the leg temporarily splinted Jeremy was moved to a ward. The doctor who had set Jeremy's fracture examined it again and blandly said, "Son, you'll never play football again."

Jeremy went home after his release from the hospital, and Sara, his girl, would bring over his lessons. Their conversations were subdued and listless. Jeremy just didn't have very much to say. Others from school came to visit and Jeremy's leg cast soon looked like the scribbled pages of a yearbook. News that Jeremy was through with football and that his scholarship was worthless had buzzed up and down the corridors of Cora Puttman High. On days when Jeremy's despair was noticeable to Miss Mable, she sent the visitors away. Jeremy wanted to be alone, he had some thinking to do.

When Jeremy felt he had mastered the crutches, he was driven to school and picked up every day by his grandfather. His evenings were spent in Miss Mable's kitchen studying, with his leg resting on a pillow-cushioned chair, and listening to the radio. He heard news of a war overseas in a foreign place, news that assured America that "we were winning the war."

Later, during the summer, Jeremy hobbled around

the farm and did whatever he could to help out with the chores. His evenings were still spent listening to the radio. Military service was becoming more enticing, more exciting, as time passed. Jeremy didn't equate the word "casualty," which he heard on the radio, with bullet-riddled corpses. It was just a word to him, the real meaning did not ring through. Death is an incomprehensible shadow to the young.

Graduation night filled the auditorium with friends and relatives of the senior class. The graduation gowns were teal blue and the little tassels hanging from the caps each senior wore were a bright yellow.

After the procession of graduates had crossed the stage and after the closing speeches, the students joined their families and friends at the back of the auditorium for refreshments. Miss Mable, overwhelmed with emotion, clung to Jeremy's arm. Cousin Rory took Jeremy aside and, for the first time in his life, embraced his grandson. The embrace, a gesture completely foreign to Rory, lasted for about one second.

But it didn't take too long for all of this happiness to

subside, and Jeremy soon realized that he was discontent and restless. After two weeks of hanging around the farm and thinking about the faded rainbow that was Jackson State University, he announced that he was going to Memphis to see his mother.

Jeremy purchased his ticket, boarded the train, and found himself a nice window seat where he could look out at the scenery and think. He had a little suitcase for his clothes, which he used as a footstool. Beads of sweat dotted his forehead, and rings of perspiration formed on his shirt by his underarms.

A young man made his way up the aisle of the car that Jeremy occupied. He had a sandwich caddy hanging by two straps over his shoulders and resting against his belly. Remembering his own days of hawking sandwiches, Jeremy purchased a chicken salad on wheat bread and told the boy to keep the change.

When Jeremy disembarked in Memphis he accosted the first person he saw who looked like a resident and inquired where the military recruiting office was located. He found what he wanted and walked through the door.

He was given a written examination, which was followed by a complete physical. After passing both, he sat down in a chair on the visiting side of the metal desk of the recruiting officer in charge who was studying the results of the written exam. The man kept shaking his head, and looking up suspiciously at Jeremy, incredulous because of Jeremy's high score. Thinking that the high score might have been luck, the officer asked Jeremy to take the same exam again. The results were the same.

"Freeman, with a score like this you can pick your branch of service. Here's a list of the opportunities the armed forces — "

Jeremy cut him off. "I want to be an airborne ranger."

The recruiting officer looked at him. "Son, I don't think you've had time to make an informed decision regarding what type of service you would like to perform for your country. With scores like these, you qualify for — "

"Sergeant Wilson," Jeremy read his name off the nameplate on the desk, "I want to be an airborne ranger."

The sergeant looked at Jeremy and saw the determination in Jeremy's eyes. He looked down at Jeremy's background information and saw that he was only seventeen years old.

"Freeman, I can't sign you up for that type of service without authorization and consent from your parents or guardians."

Jeremy stood up. "I'll be back."

Jeremy went back to the recruiting office the next day with his mother, who was miserable about Jeremy's decision and wept openly. Sergeant Wilson sat on the other side of the desk and watched as Jeremy insisted that his mother sign the papers that would let him enlist in the type of service he desired.

After a bitter argument and much protest on the part of Vera, she picked up the pen in her shaking hand and signed her son's life away.

The bus, packed full of new recruits, arrives in Fort Benning, Georgia at 3:00 am. All the men are bleary-eyed with sleeplessness, feeling and seeing with the sharp clarity of exhaustion.

Bright floodlights illuminate the parade grounds where two men, dressed in khaki uniforms with Smokey the Bear Mr. Ranger hats tucked on their heads, are standing with their arms behind their backs, staring with distaste through the bus windows.

"All right you shitheads, line up," the man wearing the most stripes bellows.

Feet shuffle in confusion.

"Move it goddamn it," the man roars. "You're the stupidest bunch of candyasses I've ever seen. Move! Move!"

Jeremy stands in line with the rest. The sergeant walks up and down the line of trembling men who are paralyzed with their separate but similar fears, ranting in a booming voice.

"I'm Sergeant Paulson and I've got the tasteless and thankless job of trying to make you Girl Scouts into men. And I'm going to enjoy doing it. This is the army, this is the best thing that will ever happen to any of you."

Sergeant Paulson, six foot two, big and bad with a nose the width of a football field, singles out Jeremy and stands right in front of him.

He screams, "Do you maggots understand me?"

Jeremy's face gets sprayed with saliva, but he is so full of fear that he doesn't dare take the chance of wiping it off.

In unison, the men holler out, "Yes, Sergeant!"

Paulson starts making his way up and down the line again screaming into each face as he sees fit. "When I say go, you go. When I say stop, you stop. When I say shit, maggots, drop your goddamn fatigues and shit. Do I make myself clear?"

"Yes, Sergeant!"

Jeremy, standing there, feels alone although there must be close to one hundred other men around him. He stares straight ahead at the blackness of the night on the edge of the parade grounds. His heart is pounding, and his eyes follow Paulson as soon as the man gets anywhere near him. He is afraid not to. He feels a great welling relief every time Paulson makes his way towards the end where Jeremy is not. He thinks, "What the hell is this? What the hell have I got myself into?"

When Sergeant Paulson's battery starts running down, Mr. Clock has ticked around to 0400 hours. Although the men have been standing there for just sixty minutes, it feels to each of them like it has been all night. Their muscles hurt, their bones ache, their heads are pounding with confusion and a very real fear. Paulson gives an order for the men to pick up their belongings and follow him. Each man does his best to keep up with Paulson's pace.

Jeremy enjoys the feel of running and finally being able to move out of the stand-at-attention position he has been in for the last hour. He starts to get excited and curious about what is going to happen to him next. The men are hustled into a long barracks where their personal belongings are inspected one by one by a stony-faced officer behind a long metal table. Cigarettes, after shave, vitamins, driver's licenses, and the like are all thrown into a large metal barrel. Each item's disposal is accompanied by a sneer and the comment, "You won't need this where you're going, shithead."

The shithead on the other side of the table, standing

at attention, dare not disagree. When this procedure has been completed, old Mr. Clock has ticked around to 0600 hours.

Paulson tells the men to look alive, or they won't be for long, and to follow him once again. He leads them into yet another barracks where five barber chairs await them. Each head is shaven bald, each individual identity thus destroyed. Paulson now leads the men to their next destination to get outfitted with their uniforms and the other things they will need for their eight week stay. All the contents are stuffed by each man into a provided duffle bag.

Paulson leads them to their new home, the barracks where they will be living until their basic training is over.

"You shitheads got five minutes to shit, shower, and shave. Inspection is in fifteen minutes. I want you dressed, I want your bunks made correctly, and I want this goddamn barracks shipshape. Do I make myself clear, maggots?"

Each man, standing in front of the bunk that will be his own, answers loudly and with forced enthusiasm, "Yes, Sergeant!"

In fifteen minutes, as promised, Paulson conducts their first barracks inspection. Possessions not properly folded and stored in footlockers are thrown into the faces of their owners. A man standing towards the front of the barracks faints with exhaustion. Paulson lets him lie there, ignoring him while he continues his first lesson of military discipline and order.

Jeremy is standing at attention and decides that he doesn't like Sergeant Paulson at all. "I'll show this son of a bitch," he thinks, "I'm gonna make it through this and all of the other shit they throw at me."

When inspection is finally over, the men are led by Paulson to the mess hall for their first military meal. "You've got thirty minutes to eat, then I want your asses on the parade grounds for inspection and drill. Do I make myself clear?"

"Yes, Sergeant!"

Paulson departs, and the men let out their first sigh of relief. They form a line and grab a tray to make their way down the grub line being served up by Privates on KP duty. The men behind the steam counter have nothing to say. There is bacon, sausage, ham, scrambled eggs, oatmeal, pancakes, grits, dry cereal, orange juice, grapefruit juice, coffee, milk. Uncle Sam feeds the cannon fodder well. There's something in the milk, though, that the men don't know about, saltpeter. Uncle Sam doesn't want the men to concentrate on anything except the training he is providing, especially women.

The men are going about the very shy business of trying to get to know each other. After all, they are going to be roommates for a while. A black man behind Jeremy strikes up a conversation with him.

"My name's Sanford."

Jeremy shakes his hand and answers, "I'm Freeman."

"Goddamn, man, you look young. How old are you?"

"Seventeen."

"Come on, man, you're bullshitting me. They draftin' 'em this young now?"

"I didn't get drafted, I enlisted."

Sanford stares at Jeremy in confusion and finally shakes his head.

"What the hell you want to go and do that for?"

"Adventure."

"Fuck adventure, man, I want to get outta this shit."

Jeremy points out the food that he wants and the private behind the steam counter serves it up on his tray. Jeremy makes his way over to a table and sits down to eat his breakfast. He doesn't really feel like eating, but he has the good sense to force some food into himself. He starts realizing that this is going to be a long, hard day. Sanford joins him, along with some other men. Sanford starts up a conversation with a white boy as big as a house.

"Goddamn man, how the fuck you get so big?"

"I was raised up on a farm in Joja. I been workin' the fiel' since I was a young un."

Sanford turns to Jeremy and remarks, "A corn-fed honky." Jeremy keeps eating.

Sanford's attention turns back to the other man.

"What's your name, man?"

"Carter." (This comes out Caarta.)

"Well, Carter, my name's Sanford. I'm just a poor boy from Detroit. You ever been to Detroit?"

Carter answers, "Nope, never been outta Joja."

"Well, Carter, you damn sure getting out of Georgia now, we all gettin' the hell out of Georgia."

The men finish their meal and head out to the parade grounds where Sergeant Paulson stands waiting.

The men are taken on a little tour of the base, a running tour. Every time one of the men loses his cadence and steps out of line, Paulson runs up into his face and lets the man know that he is a shithead and that he will most likely die in combat. He also reminds them all that he is not their mama and they had better shape up or he will, by God, beat the living hell out of them. By dinner time, 1700 hours, the new men are completely exhausted and starving. Jeremy doesn't know where he will find the strength to pick up his fork, but hunger helps him. The dinner is spent getting to know more men. Sanford and Carter seem to be sticking pretty close and end up at the same table as Jeremy once again. Carter is muttering that the first chance he gets he is going to whip Sergeant Paulson's ass.

0500 hours rolls around all too quickly... the men are just falling into a deep, catatonic sleep. Paulson's pounding gait and louder-than-thunder voice boom the men awake from their own separate dreamlands. "Five minutes to shit, shower, and shave. I want your fucking bunks made and you maggots ready for inspection."

"Yes, Sergeant!"

One man, thoroughly overcome with exhaustion, sleeps through the tirade. Sergeant Paulson's size-twelve boot kicks the foot of the man's bunk, the boom resounds all over. He sits up wide-eyed and confused, fear washes over his features and his bladder lets go. He jumps up from his cot, shamefaced.

Feet shuffle, then run. The men break for the large shower room and count the minutes off in their heads. Underarms, genitals, and feet are washed, the other body parts are ignored. The races continue to the latrine section of the barracks, urinals used and side-by-side toilets occupied by grunting men. There's no privacy in Uncle Sam's Army. The minutes are ticking, and constipation is no excuse for tardiness.

Down the homestretch the men go, bunks are made and possessions stowed away in footlockers. The men quickly don their uniforms and stand at attention at the foot of their bunks waiting for inspection. It comes. Bunks with the slightest wrinkle are torn apart and the owner is humiliated in front of everyone. T-shirts not tucked in properly are ridiculed. After much torment, tearing down, and tearing apart, and yelling "you shitheads are not at home... your mother can't keep house for you now... from the way you make your bunk, I bet that she didn't do nothin' but whore around... " the men are led out to the parade grounds to begin their day of marching, lectures, and drill.

After running five miles and two hours of drill in formation, the men are led to bleachers in the open air under the hot Georgia sun. An officer with rows of ribbons pinned to his chest is standing behind a podium readying his notes for his lecture on jungle warfare. He, after all, has been there. A Vietnam veteran getting ready to teach the recruits what it takes to survive in the jungle, according to Uncle Sam. His mouth purses with distaste as he thinks about what it really takes. A lot of goddamn luck and a lot of goddamn killing, but his superior officers wouldn't take too kindly to him telling these pasty-faced motherfuckers the truth. He wants to be a lifer in the military, he doesn't know if he'll make it... the fucking nightmares...

He starts talking, his voice droning on and on, blasé and dull, lulls Jeremy. The hot sun beating down against his neck acts as an additional sedative. Jeremy's eyes get heavy and his chin starts pressing against his chest. He senses the presence of someone very close to him, he feels like all eyes are turned on him, he jolts awake.

Jeremy opens his eyes and sees Sergeant Paulson standing in front of him. He stares. Sergeant Paulson's baseball bat-sized finger pokes Jeremy's chest hard right over his heart. Jeremy feels like it penetrated and that blood will start running down his chest.

"How," Sergeant Paulson drones the word out so it seems like he is saying it for five minutes, "would you like to have a Purple Heart?"

"Heart" is said so loud that all others getting ready to nod, on the far end of the bleachers, sit up straight and concentrate on trying to pay attention.

Jeremy starts sweating.

Paulson says it again, even louder, "How would you like to have a Purple Heart?"

"I wouldn't, Sergeant," Jeremy says.

"Pay attention then, maggot." Jeremy feels like all the men sitting around him can feel the vibrations from his fear.

After Paulson feels that his point is well taken, he joins the man by the podium. He folds his arms in front of his chest and keeps an eye on the bleachers. The men fight their exhaustion to stay awake.

In a week or so, Jeremy starts picking up on some of Sergeant Paulson's favorite sayings and entertains the other men in his barracks by imitating Sergeant Paulson and the inspections that he imposes on them all.

One evening in the barracks, as men are writing letters to sweethearts, mothers, and friends, while others are playing cards and listening to the radio and telling tall tales about their exploits and love affairs back home, Jeremy is prancing around in front of Sanford, Carter, and the others that form the clique around him.

"All right, you maggots," Jeremy booms, "I want you dressed in five minutes, that's five minutes, maggots, to shit, shower, and shave. I want you Girl Scouts out on the parade grounds and I want you spit shined and clean... "

Jeremy doesn't see Carter pointing, motioning for him to stop, and goes right on. "I want you maggots to run, run, run... "

For the second time, Jeremy feels that imposing presence. He turns and sees Sergeant Paulson standing there. The barracks gets very quiet. Paulson instructs Jeremy to follow him and takes him on a nighttime running tour of the base, five miles. When they get to the edge of the parade grounds, Paulson picks up a conveniently located entrenching tool and instructs Jeremy to dig.

"You're digging your grave, shithead. Six by three by six. I want you to keep saying, like you did when you were running for your life, 'I'm an agitating imitator.'"

Jeremy complies, "I'm an agitating imitator... I'm an agitating imitator... I'm an agitating imitator... "

After Jeremy completes the assignment, Sergeant Paulson removes a kitchen match from his shirt pocket and lights one of the stinky cigars he is always smoking when off duty. After the cigar glows nicely, he shakes the match out and throws the stick into the hole.

"Bury it, maggot."

Basic Training... Jeremy and the other men learn how to march, they learn the military chain of command, they learn how to obey orders, they learn how to drill, they learn that they are doing a great service for their country, they learn that they are extraordinary.

Their 0300 hour arrival was intended to disorient them. It worked. Sergeant Paulson scared some, and motivated others, like Jeremy, into a killing frame of mind. He successfully took away their individuality and made them all focus on the group. He became the enemy and made them focus their hatred on him, thus binding them together with that common denominator. By the time Paulson finished, Jeremy was slobbering with motivation and was ready to proceed to the next step, Advanced Infantry Training.

The training is intended to destroy a man's personality and rebuild it, to convince the men to be ready to die before being dishonored. If you tell a man he is extraordinary in an extraordinary situation over and over, he will act accordingly. The constant drilling will instill obedience and will bind the men together as a unit, a fighting unit. The constant repetition will ensure that a soldier can load his weapon and fire in a disoriented situation without even thinking about what he is doing or why. Discipline is crucial... proven "absolute obedience" is the time-honored way of melding the individual into the group. When the men start thinking like a group, a unit, they will fight harder to maintain it. Ultimately, they will die for it...

Jeremy and his barracksmates, after completing their basic training, get onto another bus that will take them farther inside the government installation of Fort Benning. Sergeant Paulson is standing on the outside, having completed his duty, because he is expected by his commanding officer to see his men off. He's proud of the men, they've come a long way, but he'd die before he would show it.

Jeremy is sitting by a window toward the back of the bus, all the men know what he's planning to do, he told them all back in the barracks. They are waiting in nervous silence. As the driver boards the bus and turns the engine over, Jeremy flies into action. He stands and squeezes the two levers that will let him pull the window down.

Jeremy yells, "Paulson, Paulson, he's our leader, he's the one who sucks our peders!"

Paulson stares straight at Jeremy.

Jeremy stares right back at him but is praying inside that the bus will move. It does. Jeremy sits down and is loudly congratulated by the other men.

The bus rolls along and finally stops. Sergeant Peterson, the man who will be in charge of the men's Advanced Infantry Training, is there to meet them.

The men line up without being told, they have been drilled and trained well by Sergeant Paulson. The discipline already exists.

"What you candyasses just went through is nothing compared to what you're capable of doing. You'll learn how to handle your weapon, how to survive in combat situations and, most important, how to kill the enemy. I want you men to report to your barracks, stow your gear, and have your asses back here by 1400 hours on the dot."

"Yes, Sergeant!"

The men are led over to the target range. Each man is issued an M-14, a very unsophisticated rifle. After brief instructions in how to load, etc., Uncle Sam wants to scrutinize the talent. Jeremy waits for his turn and, when the men in front of him complete their rotations, he walks up with his weapon ready. He receives his instructions: fire in the standing, crouching, then prone positions. He complies.

The sergeant in charge of the men on the firing range calls in for Jeremy's scores. A reply comes over the PRC-25, "Bull's eye."

"What the hell do you mean bull's eye? Bull's eye what, standing, crouching, or prone?"

"All of the above, Sergeant."

"Bullshit. Soldier, what's your name?"

"Freeman, Sergeant!"

"Try it again, Freeman."

"Yes, Sergeant!"

The sergeant calls in again and the results are the same. "Bullshit. Where'd you learn to shoot like that, soldier?"

Jeremy is embarrassed, he thinks that everybody can shoot like he can. He answers, "I hunt a lot, Sergeant."

The Sergeant grabs an M-16 and quickly demonstrates how to load, and how to handle the weapon effectively. Jeremy watches the demonstration closely. He takes the weapon in his hands, feeling confident that he can use it.

"Try it now, Freeman." The sergeant smiles. This time it won't be so easy.

The score comes in: "Bull's eye."

The sergeant shakes his head.

Jeremy is awarded the expert, sharpshooter, and marksman medals and is earmarked right then and there for frontline combat.

The men split up into Company A and Company B and engage in mock combat situations. They belong to opposing armies and are instructed to search and destroy and capture the enemy. A Company, the one that Jeremy is in, scores the most casualties against the enemy. Sergeant Peterson tells B Company that they are dead meat, that they had better shape up because in real combat they won't be getting a second chance.

The men are taken through obstacle courses with real bullets whizzing over their heads, where they crawl on their bellies through mud under barbed wire. They climb huge walls and cross a river on a rope suspended from bank to bank. The men are expected to carry their weapon with them at all times, they are expected to carry supplies on their backs in a rucksack, they are being toughened up for what will happen to them in the jungle, toughened up to become grunts. The men are taught basic combat maneuvers, drilled over and over again to ensure their blind obedience, drilled over and over again that they are to kill the enemy.

The training is soon over and Jeremy packs his gear to be relocated to where Uncle Sam trains his men to become paratroopers. Other men, men who have no desire for further training, receive their orders. Southeast Asia.

Jump school begins with the announcement that anyone caught walking when not in the barracks or mess hall will receive severe punishment. There's no mention of what the punishment will be, and no one really wants to know or find out. The men are expected to run all the time to build up their leg muscles, so when they hit the ground after jumping out of the C-130 their legs will be strong enough to withstand the shock of the impact in the event that they do not properly execute their parachute landing fall, PLF.

Freeman — he is beginning to think of himself that way and not as Jeremy any longer — is the youngest man in the training group. The training is very rigorous and as it advances men start dropping out. Spit and polished sharp is very much emphasized here. You must be so at all times, or else. Nobody wants to find out what "else" is. The boots worn by Freeman and the other men here are unlike the ones they wore in Basic and AIT. Instead of the over-the-ankle boots, they now wear boots that lace up to right below the knee, paratrooper boots.

Training, part one, begins on a four-foot platform with a panel in front that has a door cutout shaped like the door of a C-130. The men take turns over and over exiting through the door to learn the proper way to execute their PLFs. Botched landing falls are ridiculed and comments made about stupid motherfuckers breaking their legs when it comes down to the real thing. When not practicing their PLFs, run, run, run, see the men run...

The men advance to the eight-foot platform to practice and master their PLFs. Run, run, run, see Freeman run...

Freeman climbs the wooden ladder that will take him to the platform up on the 34-foot tower. There is a harness waiting there for him. A strong rubber line is connected to the harness and the tower. Freeman steps off and falls straight down, the rubber line snaps him back up to the top simulating the shock he will feel when the real chute opens as he exits the C-130. Freeman's eyes are beginning to change. They are not soft and brown anymore.

The men run in their line formation...

"I want to be an airborne ranger, I want to live the life of danger."

The Sergeant calls out, "Sound off… "

The men reply, "One, two… "

"Count it on down… "

"Three, four… "

"Sound off… "

"One, two, three, four… one, two."

"Nine to the front six to the rear, honey, honey; nine to the front six to the rear, baby, baby; nine to the front six to the rear, that's the way we do it here, honey oh baby mine."

"Give it your left your right your left, give it your left your right your left… "

"I'm so glad, I'm in the USA, yes I'm so glad, I'm in the USA; we march up hills, and we march down hills, they teach us how to fight and kill; oh look at me, I'm in the infantry, I'm willing to die for your liberty; and if I die, on the old drop zone, just box me up and ship me home; and pin my wings upon my chest, and tell my father I done my best; and tell my mom, when it's over and done, you tell my mother I'm still her son."

"Give it your left your right your left, give it your left your right your left… "

Four men are harnessed into four open chutes connected by four separate steel clawlike arms to the 250-foot tower. It looks like an umbrella that has lost its canvas. The tower is activated and the four men are pulled up to the top, the tower releases and the men experience their first free fall. Jump, jump, jump, see Freeman jump...

The jump master, with 127 jumps to his credit and 127 insignias on his chest to prove it, is harnessed inside the door of the C-130 and is hanging out of the gaping door of the aircraft. He is cracking jokes that are funny to him at least.

"Hook up, Girl Scouts."

The man behind Freeman attaches Freeman's static line, and the man behind him connects his, all in a row, the click is the most final thing any of these men have ever heard. All the lines are attached to the steel cable, they are all waiting for the green light to go on over the door that means exit the aircraft.

"Who's number thirteen today?" the jump master asks.

"Bauer, sir!" the unlucky man screams.

"Bauer, you're gonna die, your chute ain't gonna open."

The jump master laughs uproariously.

Freeman is number three and he is swimming in fear. He feels the beads from his underarms drip down his sides and stop by the waistline of his fatigue pants. "God," he thinks, "what if... don't even think like that

Freeman, don't even think… "

The green light goes on.

The number one man in line, a lifer, who had decided he wanted to add this specialty to his military service record, suddenly changes his mind. "I'm not going to jump." His eyes look like the eyes of a doe standing in the middle of a highway with a car speeding toward it at 60. Too scared to move, too scared to blink.

The jump master has a different idea. He grabs the man by the collar, pushes him toward the door, and helps him exit the aircraft with his boot in the man's ass.

Number two jumps, Freeman jumps.

His chute opens, the shock he feels is at least twice as hard as that in the simulator, then Freeman starts to float.

"God, it's beautiful." He looks down and sees the ground approaching rapidly. There are men floating out of the sky and some are enjoying it. Others are terrified and can't wait to hit the ground. Some of the men do not, all of a sudden, want to be paratroopers anymore. Freeman does, and after completing four more jumps he earns his wings and receives his diploma and proceeds to the next stage of training.

Freeman and the other men in ranger training learn how to survive when the odds are stacked against them, radically stacked against them. Freeman and the other men become killers, government-trained assassins whose objective is to kill as many NVA, as many of the Enemy, as possible.

Freeman and the other men learn how to hump. Kill, survive, kill, survive, kill, survive, this is drilled into Freeman's head over and over and over and over.

Hand-to-hand combat techniques are demonstrated and learned. Freeman learns how to kill a man with his bare hands. He is a professional soldier, a professional product of Uncle Sam's hit men, he is a hit man himself.

Freeman is slobbering with complete motivation, killing motivation.

He completes his six-week ranger course and receives his orders. The destination is not Frankfurt, Germany, what he had put in for. Freeman's destination is Southeast Asia.

Woosh Thump Woosh Thump Woosh Thump Woosh Thump… Choppers coming from the jungle into the rear to drop off the wounded and dead, and to pick up a fresh load to return to the jungle. Woosh Thump Woosh Thump Woosh Thump… A Company receives their orders: get your gear, head over to supply and get as many clean socks as you can fit into your ruck, keep in mind that your C-rats, ammo, and other survival necessities have to fit in there too. You never know how long you are going to be out there or where you are going, or when and if you are coming back…

man I been waitin for this wonder what its gonna be like out there guy back there told me to tie one of my dogtags to my left boot and the other to my right said so if I get my head blown off therell still be my tags left on my feet even if I lost one foot he said wouldnt make no difference said dont mean nothin looks just like the woods out there back home cept for its thicker them two guys hanging half way out the door of this chopper she tilts their asses be right out there in the wild blue yonder wonder when this chopper gonna land seems like they takin us to north vietnam man that white dude over there looks scared green his first time out too wonder if I look like that his eyes remind me of them rabbits I use to shoot back dont think about that freeman dont mean nothin I like that dont mean nothin

"Jeezuss Christ, I got me a whole goddamn bunch of fresh picked cherries here. All right you cheese-dicks, listen up. This ain't no motherfuckin' AIT, and this ain't no motherfuckin' ranger training, this is motherfuckin' Nam. You fuck it up out here it's your ass. You do somethin' stupid and you'll get a trip out of the damn bush in a bag, a fuckin' black body bag. Motherfuckers back at the CP said there ain't too much Enemy activity out here, only thing them motherfuckers know is how to jag off. We go 1,500 meters and dig in, fuckin' ambush."

what the hell we supposed to do I guess I better stick as close to that guy as I can sounds to me like he knows what hes talkin about anyway man this shit is thick remember what they said about not usin my hands to part the foliage them snakes that the dinks hang up there them little suckers that bite right between the fingers on the webbing of my hand they call them two steppers two steps youre dead shit

"Well, well, look what we got us here Cherry, we got us a dead dink. Son of a bitch stink, don't he?"

maggots crawling out the guys stomach wonder how long god I hate to puke

"L.T.'s got a dead man back there, want's to call it in on the PRC-25."

"What's your name, soldier?"

"Freeman, sir."

"I ain't no goddamn sir, name's Sonny. You come through that bush all by yo'self?"

"Yeah."

"First time out?"

"Yeah."

"Next time a motherfucker tell you to do somethin' like that, tell 'im to get fucked, you hear? 'Less you stupid enough to volunteer for it. That motherfucker back there ain't no lieutenant, he crazy, you dig where I'm comin' from, blood?"

"Yeah."

"No, the fuck you don't, cherry. Motherfucker think he gonna live forever, he been here so goddamn long don't know nothin' but Nam. Don't do nothin 'less it feels right inside your belly, do what your motherfuckin' belly be tellin' you. You get me, man?"

"Let's move out, see what that crazy motherfucker Conner lucked up on."

this shit is crazy its real dying oh god please dont let that happen to me I promised grandma Id come home I wonder if all these other guys are thinkin like stop stop listen look whats that oh god I killed him up in the tree he was gonna shoot somebody one of us

Slap.

I killed a man and he slaps me on my motherfuckin back

"Hey, Pauly, you owe Freeman one of them motherfucker's ears, gook was gonna shoot your ass."

Laughter.

"I don't want one, he's dead, why don't you leave him alone?"

"Hey Bro, cool out, don't mean nothin'."

this shit is for real got to keep lookin and listenin all the time motherfuckers slick as shit a man oh shit I killed a man dont mean nothin fuck it dug in good trip flares and claymores set its quiet god too quiet not knowing getting dark charlie like the night god the worst part is not knowing whats going to happen Id rather shit

Freeman jumps.

"My name's Tony, friends call me Doc."

"Don't want no friends."

"What's your name man?"

"Said I don't want no friends."

"Don't have to be my motherfuckin' friend to tell me your goddamn name man."

"Freeman."

"Well, Freeman, looks like I'm sharin' the Hilton here with you. Want the first three?"

"No, I want to watch."

quiet glad he shut up concentrate listen they out there somewhere goddamn I wish something would happen

TTTTTHHHHUUUUMPPPPA The night comes alive with mortar, tracers, and rockets, white hot, deadly wasps ripping through the jungle night. Enemy fire.

"Get Colfax, Doc, he's hit... "

"I ain't goin' out there man."

Oh say can you see, by the dawn's early light. What so proudly we hailed, at the twilight's last gleaming.

Another round explodes close, Doc and Freeman bury their faces in the dirt.

O'er the rockets' red glare, the bombs bursting in air.

Gave proof through the night, that our flag was still there.

"I'll get him motherfucker."

jesus somebody fuck it stay down low freeman stay down real motherfuckin' low

"Hey Colfax, I'm here, I got you man. Stay down low, man, I'm gonna pull you in."

"That you, cherry?"

"Name's Freeman."

"Am I gonna die?"

"No man, you'll be all right, just stay down. Gonna drag you in, you gonna make it."

"Yeah."

Quiet. Charlie goes to sleep.

"Fix him up, motherfucker."

"Hey Freeman, I… "

"Fuck you, Doc."

"Gonzales, call for a medevac on the PRC-25, Colfax is hit."

"Iz prick-25 Freeman, prick-25, comprende?"

Woosh Thump Woosh Thump Woosh Thump. The night explodes as the chopper is hit by an Enemy rocket. Shrapnel and fire rain into the jungle, quickly extinguished by the monsoon.

Woosh Thump Woosh Thump Woosh Thump.

Freeman and Doc stand there looking at each other, eye to eye, hate is spitting out of Freeman's like silver needles from Fourth of July sparklers, from Doc's there is questioning wonder, amazement, and shame.

"You ain't doin' your job, motherfucker."

Freeman's finger pokes Doc's chest hard, right over his heart. Doc stumbles back with the force of it. Freeman persists.

"You're not doin' your motherfuckin' job, motherfucker."

"Man, they was shootin' and shit, I could'a got hit."

"Fuck that. How'd you like your honky ass layin' out in the motherfuckin' bush and have some pussy ass motherfucker not do his fuckin' job?"

"Man, they was shootin'… "

"Fuck you white boy."

Freeman turns, after squelching the urge to spit into Doc's face, and goes back to the barracks where the heads are. Aretha Franklin is bellowing out a tune on the stereo the heads have set up like an altar, where pictures of well-lubricated, naked women are tacked up on the wall. The air is thick with the sweet, cloying smoke of wild jungle reefer. The heads take turns giving each other hits out of the disassembled barrel of an M-14. After taking a hit, Freeman makes his way through the dimly lit barracks toward the back where his cot and footlocker are located. When he reaches his cot he gently removes his .45 from his belt line and places it on the olive-drab army-issue blanket that is stretched taut on his cot. He then unslings his M-16 from his shoulder and places it with the other weapon. Freeman sits down and begins breaking each weapon down to its component parts, handling each like a loving father would the pins on his baby's diaper.

"Hey Freeman, catch."

The can of hot Black Label beer makes its way through the dense smoke end-over-end, glittering when it catches the light, and is snatched out of the air by Freeman.

"Thanks, Spike."

When Freeman pulls the ring tab, warm fuzzy beer spouts out of the hole like a whale gone crazy. Freeman plugs it with his lips and feels the gush funnel down his throat.

His head is pleasantly buzzing and the pumped-up adrenalin of Freeman's first three-week ambush experience is slowing down to near normal. There is no thought. Thinking hurts too bad. Each weapon component dances through his fingers like cards in a magician's as he caresses it with the oily rag.

"Hey white boy, you got the wrong barracks, they playin' the hillbilly music across the way."

Strong laughter, intermingled with deep ridicule, dances along with Aretha's swooning voice, as the men look over with anger at Doc.

"I want to see Freeman."

Doc stands his ground defiantly.

Spike, an ebony colored, six-foot-two brother, is standing on his own turf and has it in his mind not to budge. "That so? S'pose he don't wanna see your lily-white ass?"

"How the fuck you know unless you ask him, mother-fucker? Where's he at?"

Freeman is catching the confrontation but he doesn't want any company, especially Doc's. He remembers Colfax lying out there screaming, the blood pouring out of his stomach where the bullets entered, and Doc crouching down in the hole with his medical supplies ignoring Colfax's screams for help. Freeman stands. His anger is rising again.

"What the fuck you want?"

Doc walks over toward Freeman, grabs two Black Labels on the way, and presents one to Freeman as he reaches him.

"I want to be your friend."

Freeman slaps away the beer and looks Doc in the eyes. "Fuck you."

He sits down and ignores Doc, picking up where he left off on his weapon.

"Yeah, well, Freeman, I'm gonna be your fuckin' friend whether you like it or not."

The barracks gets quiet, except for Aretha, Freeman and Doc are the center of attention. Doc sits down on Freeman's bunk like he belongs there, Freeman ignores him and continues polishing.

Doc, nearly whispering, says, "I was scared, man. Ain't you scared when we out there?"

Freeman looks up, his eyes piercing Doc's, ready to answer Doc's honesty.

"Yeah, I'm scared. Fuck it, don't mean nothin'."

Doc bends over and picks up the beer that Freeman had knocked away. The newly offered beer is accepted.

Doc becomes a fixture in the head's barracks, he struts in there just like he belongs and there are no questions asked. The heads just think that the "crazy Italian motherfucker" wants to see Freeman again. The heads start calling Doc "blue-eyed soul brother" as they get to know him better. When Doc gets packages from his mother at home, he shares the contents with the heads in Freeman's barracks and not with the men back in his own. It doesn't take too long for Doc to move his gear over to where he really belongs. Freeman has himself a friend.

Doc and Freeman become inseparable, kind of like Heckle and Jeckle, Bonnie and Clyde, Laurel and Hardy. The times, both few and far between, when they are not in the jungle doing LRP's and are in the small towns of Vietnam getting into trouble, they quote Stan and Ollie by saying to each other, "Another fine mess you got me into."

STAND UP THERE IN LINE BOY AND LET GENERAL WILLIAM WESTMORELAND PIN THAT BRONZE STAR ON YOUR CHEST FOR HEROISM IN COMBAT FOR DISREGARDING YOUR OWN PERSONAL SAFETY BY GOING OUT IN THE MIDST OF HEAVY ENEMY FIRE TO PULL COLFAX BACK IN, LET DOC STAND THERE IN THE REAR AND YELL OUT FOR EVERYBODY TO HEAR... "IT SHOULD HAVE BEEN A SILVER STAR, ISN'T HE WHITE ENOUGH?"

Pounding the bush with a 70-pound rucksack strapped to your back, out there for weeks at a time, running low on C-rats, watching your friends die, killing the Enemy, watching your friend step on an antipersonnel mine and lose both feet, killing the Enemy, watching your friend be decapitated by an Enemy rocket, killing the Enemy, watching your friend fall into a hole that Charlie had dug and be impaled on the sharpened bamboo that Charlie had put there covered with his own shit, killing the Enemy...

gotta change my motherfuckin socks goddamn feet get jungle rot crossed that motherfuckin river man shit fuckin leech pull the fucker off my leg fuckers head busted all the way off shit gonna have to dig the cocksucker out dont mean nothin dumb cherry motherfucker I'd blow his brains out he get anywhere near me shot the fucker right in the gut man tryin to help him out the river with his 16 dont mean nothin better him than me medevac came too motherfuckin late bro died I'll blow the fuckers brains out he get anywhere near me last pair of clean socks I got man got to try to hang some of these dirty fuckers somewhere to dry C-rats taste like shit dont mean nothin those fuckers back at the CP fuckin their goddamn desks tellin us go here go there motherfuckers got no idea where charlie is they jaggin off motherfuckers liked to blow our asses all over the bush got their COS all fucked up dropped the willie pete where we were cant get nowhere through this fuckin bush shit dont mean nothin set those fuckin trips and claymores got my 16 right here let them slanteyed fuckers come man Im ready better them than me shit son of a bitch mosquitos told them fuckers we out of repellant cant get a chopper nowhere near the fuckin place jungle crawling with dinks gonna have to deal with the bloodsuckers frag their goddamn asses fuckin c rats almost gone better get a chopper through soon 297 more days and a wakeup thats all fuck it dont mean a goddamn thing

"Doc, wake your ass up man, it's your three now."

"Catch some Z's Freeman, fuckers out there man I

can smell 'em."

"Wake my ass."

"Yeah, I'll wake the whole motherfuckin' jungle man."

my three shit still nighttime dug in good folks gonna start shootin any time now better wake doc up so he be ready its so motherfuckin dark man cant see a mother-fuckin thing fuck it dont mean nothin shit doc dig baby dig hurry and drop them motherfuckin fatigues man and shit charlie blow your goddamn ass sky high fuckers back at CP better not fuck up again tell gonzales to call back on the prick-25 tell them motherfuckers our COS oops sorry guys we guess we fucked up oh well you damn sure aint gonna live forever fuck it dont mean nothin

"Get down Doc!"

shit goddamn motherfuckers blew sonnys goddamn head off man oh fuck shit shoot that fuckin gook man look out doc blow the motherfucker away man got that motherfucker doc blow the motherfuckers brains out get that 60 loaded man move it asshole you want to die got it please god let us dig into the dirt man get your ass down doc got him got that rice eatin slanteye man shit dont mean nothin its oh fuck man doc they got pauly kill the goddamn dinks man kill em

Charlie has hundreds of underground bunkers snaking their way through Vietnam. It was their turf. Underground cities. Nice little nasty surprises, monsters in jack-in-the-boxes popping up everywhere. These tunnels were used for many purposes, hospitals, munitions storage, escape routes, food caches, Enemy concealment, booby traps, the list goes on and on. You are out on a search and destroy and you happen on one of the many entrances to these underground cities, you are obligated to climb down in there with a .45 in one hand and a flashlight in the other one, with a rope tied around your waist so your buddies have an umbilical cord to hang on to. Tunnel Rat.

fuckin snakes inside charlie got more than one of us with that trick keep your goddamn hands down man charlie down here for sure I can smell him no tellin what he got waitin I ever get outta here I'll never stop your goddamn lying man you know damn sure you be the next to volunteer fuck it dont mean nothin theres some goddamn mines on the floor of this motherfucker blow my goddamn foot off aint no use waitin around fuckers know Im here gonna get their goddamn shit blown off dink got a grenade shit ones a little kid better them than me got to get out of this shit

Topside the squad was having the pleasure of entertaining some NVA and showing Charlie just what the great US of A has in store for him. Another unit had taken this hill two months ago, and had secured it, and yet another unit before that... the list is endless.

"Goddamn I got dirt and shit all in my drawers, man."

"What was down there, Freeman?"

"Nothin', man."

"What the hell were you shootin' at, man?"

"Just some goddamn rats, man, that's all."

fuck it dont mean nothin got to keep beatin this goddamn bush till we go out 2000 meters aint no tellin what we run across out there this shit is so goddamn thick I cant see a thing hey man look out thats a wire

"Conner, don't move!"

"Dumb fuckin' asshole, shit help me man, I'm fucked."

"Just stay cool man, I'll try to disarm it for… "

hit the dirt freeman fuckin shrapnel oh shit

TTTTHHHHUUUUMPPPPA Charlie hears his claymore and knows there are GI in the area. Have a little mortar boys to make your lives more interesting? How about if we move in now and see how many of you we can fuck up? We know where your other squad is too GI, we think we'll get you all fucked up here in the jungle and have you kill each other. We'll get right in the middle and then get out, have you GI's shooting each other all to hell. Friendly fire.

"Bravo six, Bravo six, this is Alpha, over." TTTTH-HHHUUUMMPA "We need beehive man, over."

Bravo six hears and sends some rounds in to the coordinates they were given. Things get quiet.

Body count. Conner got it and that new cherry, Williams. Let's go see how many NVA. Surprise, GI! Your body count is for the 2nd squad, you just wiped out your own men, your buddies.

"Shoot me man, please, don't leave me like this man." The fallen soldier lies there with no legs, he is barely alive. Freeman places his .45 against the man's temple and pulls the trigger. The body jumps.

"Hey Freeman, look what I got us man."

"Doc, you motherfucker, where in the hell did you get those?"

"Hey man, I got my fuckin' sources. Let's put these fuckers on and go have us some fun at the officer's club."

They walk in and the conversation stills. Two captains, eighteen-year-old airborne rangers who look like they were just weaned off their mother's milk. Something unheard of. Perched on top of their heads are the black berets that only rangers can wear, and the captain's insignia Doc pilfered are affixed to their olive green jackets. Most of the men inside the club are nearing thirty, most are white, and none is an airborne ranger. Strictly rear echelon here.

Doc and Freeman make their way over to the bar and order themselves a couple of boilermakers. The conversation in the background starts buzzing again.

"What was really in that hole, Freeman?"

"Fuckin' rats."

"Come on, motherfucker, I know there was something else in there."

"You callin' me a liar, motherfucker?"

"Yeah, I am."

Punches start flying. Freeman hits Doc with a good hard right and busts his lip, Doc counters and lets Freeman have it right smack in the eye. They start getting wilder, punches are flying everywhere. A captain makes the terrible mistake of trying to get in between the two and break it up. Fast as two cobras striking, Freeman and Doc grab their beer bottles and break them against the edge of the bar. They stand back to back ready to cut anybody up who tries to interfere. The bar gets quiet, the captain sits down.

"Come on, motherfuckers," Doc spits.

Freeman's and Doc's eyes have a wild look, a murderous look, then they soften. They both start laughing. They turn back to the bar and ask the bartender for another round. He refuses to serve them.

"Fuck you, motherfucker."

Doc and Freeman make their way outside the officer's club and decide they'd rather go some place else where the drinks will flow freely. They head down the street to find that other bar that promises more escape from why they are here and what they've been doing. On the way they stop at an opium den and Vietnam becomes paradise.

"I've got five motherfuckin' days and a wakeup man, ain't nothin gonna stop me from gettin' back to the World."

"Danielson, if I had five days, man, I goddamn sure wouldn't be humping this bush, man, I'd have my ass in the rear until I got my fuckin' DEROS papers."

"Doc, you know I can't leave you motherfuckers out here by yourselves, you'd get all fucked up without my ass watchin' over you."

Laughter.

"Hey man, where the fuck you get that grease gun?"

"Found it by that dead gook about 500 meters back. I'm gonna clean the motherfucker real good, break it down, and take it home as a souvenir."

"Hey Freeman, want some of this smoke?"

"Yeah."

Freeman walks over toward where Danielson and Doc are sitting, the only sounds in the jungle are the fuck-you lizards singing to each other in the trees and the splatter of rain on the leaves. Freeman sits down opposite Danielson, there is a round in the chamber of the grease-gun, the bullet whines past Freeman's head and he feels its heat against his temple. Freeman bolts to his feet and turns the barrel of his weapon on Danielson.

"You ever do that again motherfucker I'll kill you. I don't give a motherfuck if you got one day and a wakeup."

Time to pick up your ruck and strap it to your back, orders came down that a village was sighted near your present position. Search and destroy any Enemy and confiscate any munitions you may find. How can you tell who the Enemy is? You can't.

"GI, GI, GI, got food? GI, GI... "

A whole herd of emaciated, big brown-eyed children run up to you as you enter their village with their hands stretched out in hopes of them being filled with C-rats, A-rats, or anything else the good-hearted GI's will give them. Old men and women echo the plea being made by the children, and soon you are being followed like you are pied pipers of the jungle.

look out for the ones hiding their hands behind their backs might be a grenade I dont like the look of those fuckers sitting over there by that hut goddamn these kids are like a swarm of ants on a fuckin bone all over the goddamn place dont feel right theres something going on doc feels it too I can tell by lookin at him danielson just slapped that kid should have fragged him dont look right goddamn wish these little fuckers would get back

A woman with a grenade in her left hand comes running out of her hut, the children and old people scatter. The other men in the squad are standing there in confusion, Freeman sees the woman running toward him with a determined look on her face. The woman's right hand starts moving towards her left to disengage the pin.

"Hit the dirt!"

The men react and begin firing into the crowd of Vietnamese, not caring who they are hitting or why, they have all become the Enemy.

I killed her oh god Im gonna be sick

"Freeman, goddamn man, I'm thirsty. We ain't had no water for two days now."

"Fuck you, Doc, you talk about water all the goddamn time. Every time they send a chopper anywhere near this place Charlie shoots it out the damn sky."

"Man, Danielson getting it back there really fucked me around, man. He was out here past his time, man, had his DEROS papers waitin' for him back in the barracks, seems like Charlie knows when one of us is getting ready to go back to the World, seems like he be aimin' for short timers."

"Shut the fuck up, Doc, will you?"

"Where you goin', Freeman?"

"I'm goin' to go find us some water so you'll shut up."

"Man, you're crazy, Charlie all over, you'll never make it."

"Ain't got a thing to worry about, I got 219 and a wakeup. Give me your canteen and get me about five from the other men."

"Freeman, don't fuckin' do it man."

"Fuck you, Doc."

The enemy fire eases up, and the ranger squad continues to move on in the direction they were ordered to go. They come to the same river that Freeman got the water from, and they see a body lying face down in the water, the limp legs floating up and down in the gentle current.

STAND UP THERE IN LINE BOY AND LET GENERAL WILLIAM WESTMORELAND PIN THAT BRONZE STAR ON YOUR CHEST FOR HEROISM AND VALOR FOR DISREGARDING YOUR OWN PERSONAL SAFETY IN THE MIDST OF HEAVY ENEMY ACTIVITY AND VIRTUALLY SAVING ALL THE MEN IN YOUR SQUAD BECAUSE IT TAKES THEM ANOTHER WEEK TO GET THROUGH AND DROP YOU SOME WATER AND SOME MORE C-RATS AND AMMO AND YOU HAVE BEEN PINNED IN THE BUSH ALL THAT TIME, LET DOC STAND THERE IN THE REAR AND YELL OUT FOR EVERYBODY TO HEAR... "IT SHOULD HAVE BEEN A SILVER STAR, ISN'T HE WHITE ENOUGH?"

You've been ordered to go out 1,500 meters with the

other men in your squad. You have your medic, RTO, M-60 machine-gunner, lieutenant, and the other men with their various specialties. The lieutenant asks for a volunteer to take point, to be the first man through the bush to confront whatever Charlie has in store. Point man.

Freeman volunteers, Freeman always volunteers.

An NVA soldier and Freeman are standing six feet away from each other. The NVA has his AK-47 barrel pointing directly at Freeman's heart. In contrast, Freeman's M-16 is pointing at the jungle floor. Both men... Enemies... stare each other down. The NVA's finger is on the trigger, Freeman feels like his might as well be up his ass.

Im dead oh fuck

Neither man has reached his twentieth birthday. Men children. Enemies. As their eyes remain locked a communication is established, human communication. Questions are asked inside each man's head, "Why do I want to kill him? He never did anything to me."

The NVA slinks off into the jungle, snakelike, silent. For some unknown reason he spares Freeman, the eyes, the soul windows, "Go home black man, this is not your war," the propaganda Charlie leaves lying around on printed flyers on the jungle floor.

It's night time again, time for more to die.
Jungle leaves are dripping, monsoon water and
      blood.

How's it feel, GI to be this far away from
        home?
Home where they call you names,
And won't let you in the white man's doors.
How's it feel, blood, laying here waiting to die?
For a country that doesn't even want you.

If you make it back, black man, try to find a
        job.
You'll sit there day after day looking at the
        sky.
What do you see, black man?
"Clouds dripping napalm, sun reflecting off
        dead men's eyes."
What do you smell, black man?
"Mortar rounds, blood, rotting bodies, death,
        death, death."

If you make it back, black man, you won't
        make it here.
You should have died for your country,
Been a good "boy" and died.
Your country doesn't want you, you don't fit
        in.
You never did, you never will.

black pajamas black pajamas motherfucker
        coulda killed me

A sniper's bullet whizzes through the jungle
foliage...

"Medic! Medic!"

"Bravo six, Bravo six, be advised, L.T. Gray is hit, man, over."

"Alpha, this is Bravo six, we copy. How bad is it, over."

"Get a fuckin' medevac in here man, is bad, over."

"Roger that, who's next in command there, over?"

"Jezus, nobody, over."

Doc rushes over to the fallen man, the leader, and sees that his services will not be needed this time. Gray would be better off with a padre. His eyes are staring straight up at the sky sightlessly through the jungle leaves. His chest is torn open and his vital fluids have soaked his camouflage shirt.

this is some kind of motherfuckin joke me a goddamn battlefield commissioned lieutenant I hope I dont get any of these men killed at least I got doc and gonzales on my squad all of the rest of these motherfuckers are cherries watch them motherfuckers close man theyll give all of us away got a good RTO and a good medic my machine gunner is a fuckin cherry thats all the fuck we need get into some heavy charlie and have that motherfucker crack got my M-79 I'll pull the slack if the motherfucker cant handle it lieutenant freeman in the field aint that a bitch

"Jesus Christ Doc, why the fuck you make me do that, man?"

Freeman is standing over Doc, who is lying on the floor of the barracks with his lip split open from the punch Freeman just put there. The other men in the barracks just ignore the two, by now they are used to these outbursts.

"Fuck you, Freeman, it's a fuckin' gesture, just a fuckin' Dago gesture. I was just trying to get my point across to you man, that's all."

"Ain't no fuckin' reason to slap my goddamn face, motherfucker."

"Shit, all my people do that, don't mean nothin'."

"Doc, we don't have a motherfuckin' thing in common, you know that?" Freeman reaches down to offer Doc his hand to help him up, Doc accepts. "Man, you grew up in the fuckin' Bronx and I'm a goddamn country boy. Did you really have a coop full of pigeons on the roof of your building?"

"Yeah."

They sit down together on Freeman's cot. "I use to stay up there a lot when I wasn't in the streets, use to dream about being a doctor."

Freeman grunts.

A very agitated cherry staggers into the barracks and

sits down quickly on his cot. He puts his face into his hands and his shoulders start jerking up and down.

"What the fuck is wrong with you, shit for brains?"

He looks up and wipes his eyes. "Man, did you hear what happened to McCall, man?"

All the men look at the cherry waiting for him to go on.

"Man, he was in Saigon on R&R — "

Freeman interjects, "Fuckers try to send my ass to fucking Saigon on R&R I'll frag their goddamn asses."

Laughter.

"McCall man, he wanted to get laid, you know. He got himself a broad and, oh shit man, he got himself a broad and the bitch got him with a goddamn razor."

"Freeman, I want you to take the first squad and secure that clearing over to the east, about 200 meters out."

"No."

"What did you say, Lieutenant?"

"No, sir."

"I'm gonna Article 15 your ass for that, that's a direct order, Freeman."

"Fuck you. I said no, sir, and I mean no."

Doc is standing in the background, catching all of this.

"Frag the cocksucker, Freeman. I didn't see a fuckin' thing."

Doc brings his M-16 up and points it in the Lieutenant's direction. Lieutenant Lockhart, fresh out of OCS, is visibly shaken. They didn't have anything in the training manual about this.

"Freeman, I'm going to give you one more chance. Take your squad out and — "

Freeman cuts him off. "Fuck you."

Freeman's men, his RTO, medic, M-60 machine gunner, and his riflemen all sit there waiting to see what their leader will do. He doesn't budge. Neither will they.

Lockhart turns to the second squad and gives them the order that Freeman refuses to obey.

TTTTHHHHUMMPAAAAAAAA The Enemy, after hitting the clearing with mortar, penetrates and wipes out all of the men on the second squad. A man lies there wounded, pretending that he's dead, and is quickly obliged by the bullets of an Enemy AK-47. There is blood and death and mortar smells, there are no survivors from the second squad.

Lockhart sits there with his head cradled between his two shaking hands, "How did you know man?"

"I knew, motherfucker, write my goddamn ass up, don't mean nothin'."

He shakes his head, "No." He says, "How did you know?"

"Bangkok was fucking great man, there are broads that... "

"Man, Freeman, you was lucky you was gone man, the whole 173rd got wiped out."

"Where's Doc, Gonzales, and Wilcox?"

"Doc and Wilcox are back in the barracks, man, Gonzales is in a fuckin' body bag. You lucked out, man, damn near the whole 173rd got wiped out."

The sky soldier walks away with his hands inside his fatigue pockets. There is a look of fear and confusion on his face, he shakes his head trying to deny all that has happened, those men were his friends too.

"Doc?" Freeman runs into the barracks, frightened by what he had just been told, he hopes to something, but not to God — his faith in Him is dwindling — that the troop who told him about the 173rd had his information right about Doc. "Doc?"

Doc stands up and Freeman runs into his arms, they embrace. "What the fuck happened, man?"

"Bad shit, man, a whole goddamn regiment, the fuckin' place was crawlin' with dinks."

"Where's Wilcox, Doc?"

"Freeman, the son of a bitch is over there readin' his

Bible, man, like nothin' happened."

Doc and Freeman sit down on the floor of the barracks, they lean against each other back to back, the backs of their heads resting against each other, their eyes closed. All the others inside the barracks know that these two guys have been here forever and that they want to be left alone.

Dear Jeremy... This is the hardest letter I ever had to write in my life, but I have to do it anyway. I don't quite know where to start but I guess I'll start by saying it's been so long since I've heard from you. It's been so hard for me to sleep at night, but it's even harder during the day because I know it's nighttime over there. I guess I'll get right to the point. Do you remember Ron Jackson? This is so hard — but we have been seeing each other for the past two months and he asked me to marry him last night. It was the hardest decision I ever had to make in my life because I kept seeing your face. I said "yes" and we'll be married in a couple of months. I die inside waiting for you to come home because I believe in my heart that you never will. I can't wait for you any longer because I can't wait for the impossible to happen. I don't want to know when the telegram comes home that says you are dead. Please forgive me, Jeremy, but I'm not as strong as I thought I could be when you left. I have to get on with my life, so I guess that this is goodbye. You'll always have a very special place in my heart. Love, Sara.

"Hey Freeman, I got a package from home, man, you'd better get your ass over here and get some of it while you can."

"Fuck you, Doc."

"Freeman, where you goin', man?"

"None of your motherfuckin' business. Do you have to know every time I take a shit, man?

Freeman storms out of the barracks.

In a few minutes, Freeman returns. "Did you save me something good from that package, Doc?"

Doc hands Freeman a can of fruit cocktail and three homemade chocolate chip cookies he had stashed away.

"Damn, Doc, this shit will taste even better after a couple of hits. Where's the shotgun?"

They take turns sucking on one end and blowing on the other.

The jungle is a beautiful place with all the birds singing overhead, along with the fuck-you lizards calling to each other from their tree perches. It's colorful, brilliantly lush greens and bright yellows, everything all tangled together and growing wild. It's a rain forest, where trees grow so tall that they seem to be reaching up like green pillars holding up the canopy of the sky. It's deadly. There are huge snakes, small vipers and insects that will make a man's arm swell to twice its normal size if bitten. The foliage is so thick that it's like looking at a green brick wall twined with tree branch mortar. To proceed, you have to cut through that wall without knowing what is on the other side. During monsoon the jungle floor becomes slippery, like the leeches that inhabit the raging rivers. Mosquitos breed now and wait for the dry season to go on their annual hunts, mate, and die. And there's the bigger Enemy in this jungle... Charlie is here waiting and on patrol himself.

"There's bou-coup movement here, man."

Freeman, Doc, Mehall, Wilcox, and six cherries who look like they are about to puke are taking a nice little helicopter ride past the 38th Parallel, known otherwise as the DMZ, the dividing line between North and South Vietnam. The four mentioned are dangling their legs out of the chopper's doors and the cherries' thoughts are filled with fears much like those Freeman had on his first chopper ride into the jungle.

The cherries are still a trifle green from their experience in the bush. Mehall and Wilcox captured an NVA soldier on their last ambush and they took him for a ride on the Huey. The four vets kept slapping the dink around and eventually Freeman pushed him out of the open door of the airborne chopper. The four vets laughed uproariously as the cherries paled.

Past the DMZ, although we are not supposed to be there, the chopper pilot has motioned for his cargo to prepare to rappel to the area below. The men inside the chopper check each other's rucks and ensure that they are balanced on their backs. The men prepare and wait for one word, "Go."

Like awkward two-legged spiders, they make their descents from the hovering chopper above them. The large, green insect, with its peculiar wings that rotate above its body, is giving birth once again in Charlie's jungle.

Nice of you to come over and play boys.

Freeman leads. "Lock and load."

The men follow their leader, who is serving as point man, through the pathway he creates for them. The men are spaced five meters apart from each other in line, the approximate killing radius of a grenade. Freeman takes every precaution known to him to ensure their survival.

Freeman checks his compass, looks around, and likes the feeling he gets in his gut from the immediate surroundings.

"All right you cheese-dicks, dig in, fuckin' ambush."

The men busy themselves with digging holes and filling sandbags with the materials they excavate. Trip wires are arranged around the perimeter, and claymores are set up to secure the men inside their jungle womb.

Doc and Freeman are side by side, alert and anxious for some action.

"You sure that sorry shit for brains Splendoria can handle that fuckin' claymore man?"

Freeman lights a Marlboro, cupping the match flame with his hand, "The motherfucker better or I'll... "

A rocket hits close and explodes, shrapnel flies every where, red-white hot metal fragmentation aiming to do damage to whatever it hits. Bullets, hot and angry, fly through the perimeter looking for any target that gets in their way.

The first squad is firing back into the jungle in the direction from which the conflagration is coming.

"Medic! Medic!" Wilcox screams as the cherry in the hole with him is hit by two rounds from an AK-47.

Doc makes the motion to spring up and answer the call, Freeman sees him out of the corner of his eye and attempts to stop him, "Doc, NO!"

Too late. Doc is decapitated when an Enemy rocket hits him above the sternum. His head, with the eyes still open and glassy like marbles, goes flying into the bush behind the hole his now lifeless body is lying in. Freeman goes crazy.

He looks over and sees the blood spurting out of the artery where Doc's neck used to be. An animal scream of pure rage cascades up and out of Freeman's belly, "AAAArrrrrrrgggggggghhhhhhhhh!"

Freeman springs up and runs to retrieve Doc's head

behind him. He returns with it dripping and tries to stop the flow of blood still coming out of what used to be Doc's neck. He tries to put the head back on the body.

Bullets keep coming and Freeman is unaware of the hot fire just above him. He is thrown into a deeper fit of murderous rage. The primal scream breaks loose again, "AAArrrrggggggghhhhhhh!"

In the next hole over, Mehall sees Freeman rise and begin to run toward where he believes Charlie is hiding. All he can think or feel is the need to avenge his friend. Mehall races over and clouts Freeman on the back of his neck with the butt of his .45.

"Freeman, you lucky motherfucker, your DEROS papers are here man, all you got to do is go get the motherfuckers."

Freeman is lying on his cot, his fingers laced behind his head, staring up at the ceiling of the barracks. He looks over at Ligurotis, the troop who just gave him the "good" news, and the latter sees a look in Freeman's eyes and shakes his head to deny what he has seen. There is hatred there, blank, inhuman, cold hatred.

Ligurotis thinks, "I wouldn't want to be in that motherfucker's squad."

Freeman sits, rubs his face with his hands, and straightens his tired shoulders so they are militarily erect. He stands, grabs his M-16, and walks out of the barracks toward personnel where his papers will be.

Wilcox looks up briefly from his Bible, then quickly picks up on the passage he was reading before the interruption. Mehall sits with his 16 cradled across his lap and watches Freeman leave the barracks. He says, "That motherfucker gonna re-up, man."

None of the men says anything.

The stereo is turned on and so are the men when they start popping tops and shotgunning each other. Time to party, at least they have the rest of the day and night; they don't really know how much time they have, they could be ordered out any minute, but they'd rather be fucked up when the time comes anyway.

The dark intensity in the atmosphere created by Freeman is gone with his departure, the troops decide it's time to unwind. The party is going strong, the shotgun is being loaded and refilled, when Freeman walks through the door of the barracks. Things get quiet, the eyes of the vets who know him well follow his progress.

"Is the motherfucker gonna grab his shit?" Mehall thinks. He looks over toward Wilcox and reads the same question in his eyes.

Freeman, when reaching his bunk, props his M-16 within arm's reach and lies down. The fingers become laced behind his head again.

A cherry, Patrick Bryant, walks over to Freeman

with a full bowl of smoke.

"Hey, L.T., you want some of this shit, man?"

Freeman sits, takes the offered pipe and inhales deeply. He looks Bryant in the eyes as he continues to inhale the smoke. Bryant starts feeling uncomfortable and his eyes rove around the barracks. The eyes of the vets are upon him, and he suddenly wishes he had left the L.T. alone. He looks back into Freeman's eyes and doesn't see any emotion there. They are filled with a knowledge Bryant prays to God he will never have.

STAND UP THERE IN LINE BOY AND LET GENERAL WILLIAM WESTMORELAND PIN THAT BRONZE STAR ON YOUR CHEST FOR LEADING YOUR SQUAD OUT OF THE JUNGLE DURING HEAVY COMBAT ACTIVITY AND FOR SUSTAINING MINIMAL CASUALTIES. LET MEHALL AND WILCOX STAND THERE IN THE REAR AND THINK...

"Man, don't that motherfucker ever let up man?"

"Bryant, shut your sorry ass up and hump. You're lucky you got a motherfucker like Freeman as your L.T."

"Hey, Mehall, why the fuck is he like that man? Motherfucker takes chances and goes out on patrol all by himself while we're in the fuckin' perimeter. Won't let nobody else even volunteer for fuckin' point or tunnel rat."

"He's doin' it for Doc."

"Who's Doc?"

"Shut the fuck up and hump."

The men space themselves five meters apart... an explosion rips through the jungle...

"Medic! Medic!"

Mehall is lying on the jungle floor, his legs shattered. The claymore mine effectively did its damage. Freeman rushes over to the fallen man along with the new medic assigned to the first squad.

"Motherfuck," Mehall grunts out through his pain. "Motherfuck."

Freeman tries to comfort the dying man. "Hey Mehall, you're gonna be all right."

Unknown to the troopers who make up the brigade, a mass exodus of the jungle LRP's of the 173rd is underway. When reaching their fire base, the men of Alpha, Bravo, Charlie, and Delta companies are ordered to board choppers taking them back to Bein Hoa. Upon their arrival, orders are given to supply and get outfitted with a chute and reserve. Dusk is coming over the land and pinpoints of stars begin to shine silver in the darkening sky.

Freeman is feeling the first emotion since Doc, one of pride and excitement, he is beginning to realize that he is going to be a part of something big. The men of the 173rd can hardly believe their good fortune, they are going to do what they were trained for, they are going to jump.

The men are ordered to board troop transport vehicles in a caravan that will take them to the airfield where the C-130's await their cargo. There is an intense feeling of excitement and fear in the atmosphere. The jungle seems to be a place very far away from them, yet the men know how close it really is, a matter of minutes aboard the C-130's separate them from Charlie and his jungle. The troopers disembark from the caravan and trot across the airfield to the waiting C-130's. The sky is ebony now with the brilliant stars poking holes in its blackness.

Freeman boards the C-130 and sits along the side of the aircraft's body, under the steel cable suspended overhead for the hook up of static lines, waiting for the other men to pile on. Alpha, Bravo, Charlie, and Delta are filling up the C-130's and are getting ready to take a ride.

The aircraft become airborne and slice their way through the sky of Vietnam to the destination given them by the command, Dak To. The men inside the aircraft hook up their static lines without being told. Eyes rove around searching faces and looking for a glimpse of reality. The nightmare quality of this ride is pervading all the men, they realize that they will soon be given the order to exit the aircraft. Seconds seem like minutes, minutes like hours, finally the green light over the door bursts into illumination... Freeman jumps...

goddamn Im jumpin right into the middle of a fire fight tracers going back and forth and Im right in the goddamn middle

Freeman and the other men around him are floating down into a gauntlet of hot projectiles ripping through the jungle night. The trails left by the bullets are hot white as they scratch the night sky open. As he floats, Freeman looks around him and sees that his planeload was the last to exit the aircraft and is closest to where Charlie is in the jungle. Alpha serves as point company again.

man Im gonna die

Two rounds from an AK-47 rip through Freeman's abdomen and exit through his back, one under his shoulder blade and the other just missing his heart; both have punctured a hole in his lung. Two more rounds find a target; one lodges itself by Freeman's tibia in the fatty part of his calf, the other finds his left hand and rips his thumb, leaving it dangling by a thread of skin.

As Freeman nears the ground he cradles his M-16 and rapid fires into the bush. Even near death the instinct to kill the enemy is there. As he hits the ground he releases his chute by slapping the release buttons with his one good hand. He grabs his belly and examines the blood.

Im gonna die oh man I dont want to die

Tracers are flying all around him and he hugs the ground in desperation. A fragmentation grenade explodes nearby and its metal finds Freeman's forehead. His head is split open down to his skull from right over his brow to the middle of the back of his head.

Bryant crawls up to his L.T. like an insane lizard. Upon seeing Freeman's condition he screams for help through the conflagration, "Medic! Medic!"

Freeman lies there in a stupor of pain and unreality, he resigns himself to die.

"You're gonna be all right L.T., hang in there man, the doc is comin'."

Freeman barely gets it out. "Doc?"

The medic scurries over, Doc II in Dak To, playing dodge the bullet, and loads Freeman up with pure morphine. Freeman's pain vanishes as the opiate takes hold.

"You're gonna be all right, troop, hang in there," the medic says as he applies pads of gauze and tape to the wounds on Freeman's belly. Bryant is gone, he's moved forward to pursue the enemy.

"Hang in there, man," the medic comforts. He stops the first troop he sees nearby. "Get the RTO to call back and get a medevac in here."

The troop does an about-face to comply with the request.

Two choppers are shot down before one alights nearby. Two men pile out of its doors with a stretcher to transport the wounded man back to the chopper.

feel weak feel good sorry grandma fuck it dont mean

The men run with Freeman and pile into the waiting chopper.

"Let's get the hell outta here man, Charlie all over the goddamn place."

The pilot grabs the stick and the chopper does its thing taking off into the storm. An enemy rocket glances its tail and the chopper begins to spin in answer to its force. The pilot grabs hard on the controls, saying "motherfuck."

"Move! Move! Get this one on the table." Army surgeons and nurses splattered with blood expedite the flow of bodies through the chop shop.

"Cut those fatigues off him!"

A circle of faces stare down at Freeman, the bottom halves covered in blue, with two eyes peeking out at him, then the blue continues again over the top of their heads.

"This one doesn't look too good, he's lost a lot of blood, I don't think he'll make it."

Freeman hears all the activity around him through the haze of the morphine, he wants to argue with the appraisal but cannot find the strength.

Another masked man has a different opinion, "I'm gonna try. Son, can you hear me?"

Freeman tries to respond, he can't.

"If you can hear me, son, blink your eyes twice."

Although his eyelids seem unbearably heavy, Freeman, what seems like hours later, spends the effort and blinks twice.

"He's coherent. Son, we're going to have to remove some of that blood from your chest cavity before we can operate. I want you to lay real still."

Freeman couldn't move if he wanted to. The surgeon takes a hypodermic with a twelve-inch needle and inserts it carefully over Freeman's clavicle until its point penetrates the lung. Only three inches of the needle is exposed over Freeman's skin. He pulls the plunger back and the long plastic tube fills with blood. Five times this procedure is repeated until the lung and chest cavity is relatively free from the liquid Freeman could have drowned in.

A catheter is inserted into Freeman's penis that leads up to his bladder, an incision is made in his side below the armpit and a tube is inserted there to continue the drainage of his chest and lungs. The pain is galvanizing. A mask is held over Freeman's face and he remembers no more.

An incision is made across Freeman's belly from side to side, a long jagged one that will heal to look like a lightning bolt. The damage done inside by the two AK-47 rounds is surveyed and repaired. Half of Freeman's stomach is removed, the damage so extensive that it cannot be salvaged, the same occurs with a long rope of his intestine.

"How's his BP?"

The surgeon gets his answer and continues to work.

Another surgeon is working on the jigsaw puzzle that is Freeman's left hand. "He'll probably never have full use of this again, but I think I can save the thumb."

His observation goes unnoticed. The hustle and bustle to save his life goes on around him as Freeman lies inside himself and dreams.

The crack in his head is sutured and large metal clamps are attached to the incision across his belly. An IV is administered along with several units of blood to resupply what Freeman has lost.

The surgeons have done all they can for this one, it's up to him now to do the rest. He is rolled out of the chop shop and deposited into a ward of wounded, recovering, and dying men.

Freeman wakes up wrapped in a blanket of intense agony. He cannot open his eyes because of the matter that has formed around the lids that seems to glue them together. He manages finally after much effort and lies staring up at the ceiling above him. He's in too much pain even to turn his head, he lies there concentrating all his effort on trying to remember what happened. He attempts to sit and the slight motion causes shattering pain through his abdomen. The agony in his head is a constant stabbing, while the burning in his hand seems to overshadow everything else. He starts to think that perhaps he has died and is waking up in hell.

Freeman spends the rest of his second overseas tour recovering. His new existence includes a monstrous opium habit. He makes arrangements to smuggle some home when his DEROS papers arrive.

Back to the world...

Most of the vets on the plane, which just landed at San Francisco International Airport, are looking out of the right side of the aircraft at the protestors in line with their signs, "Stop the War," "Baby Killers," "Monsters," "Murderers." There are heavily armed riot police guarding the path the men will have to take when they disembark.

The TWA jetliner's door is opened, but regardless of their long flight, the troops inside do not want to get off. The enemy is outside and they are weaponless against them.

The troops make their way to the waiting plane that will take them on the last leg of their journey, Fort Benning, Georgia. Right back to where Freeman started.

He's a lot older now, a lot wiser, a lot crazier, practically insane.

When airborne, drinks are served up, and the men start talking. "Should have fragged those motherfuckers, fuckin' Dink lovers, goddamn right."

The men fantasize with each other and wish for the familiar M-16's, M-60's, grenades, and machetes they used when humping through the jungles of Nam.

Freeman and all the other vets on the plane realize that the States will never be the same for them again.

At Fort Benning, Freeman is given sergeant stripes and his new orders read that he will be responsible for training troops who volunteer to become rangers. He is given a four-week leave and heads into town to catch a bus to Renault, Mississippi.

Miss Mable is in her kitchen, like on most other days of her life, when the back door opens quietly. Freeman stands there staring at his grandmother's back as she attends to the food simmering on top of the stove. He walks over the threshold and silently closes the door, then floorwalks across the kitchen linoleum until he is directly behind Miss Mable. He brings his hands around to the front of her face and gently covers her eyes.

"My Lord!" Miss Mable jumps in surprise.

Freeman removes his hands and Miss Mable turns around slowly.

"Baaaybeee!"

Freeman is smothered with hugs and repeated kisses all over his face. Miss Mable is sobbing tears of pure joy. Freeman is iron-hard inside her grasp. When her joy starts simmering down a bit, she feels the stiffness and steps back to look into his eyes for the answer.

What Mable sees there frightens her, she feels her knees want to give away. There's nothing in her grandson's eyes, no emotion, only quick intelligence and beneath that, cold ruthlessness. They remind Mable of a picture she saw of a wild wolf when she was a girl, a wolf who looked like he wanted to come right at your throat — his head was hunched all down low right between his forepaw blades — his mouth was open and all those razor sharp teeth he had inside — but the eyes were what she remembered the most, those eyes told you exactly what that wolf would do if you crossed his path.

Mable, holding her grandson away from herself at arm's length, says, "Sit down, baby."

Like an automaton, he pulls out a chair from the table and fits himself on it.

"I'll be right back baby, you look so thin, didn't those folks feed you none?"

"They fed me, grandma."

"I'll fix you your favorite, baby."

No response. Mable walks around behind her

grandson and pulls open the back door. On the porch there she sees the large green duffle bag that the stranger, her grandson, has brought home with him. As she stoops to pick it up by the green handles, she feels a dark presence looming behind her and sees a hand shoot out for what she was stooping for. Freeman lifts the duffle. "I'll get that, grandma. Where do I sleep?"

"Why," with much surprise, "your old room of course, baby, your room."

Freeman doesn't respond, he turns with his burden and goes down the remembered corridor.

Mable heads out back and thinks, "My Lord, my Lord, what did those folks do to my baby?"

After picking at his plate full of smothered chicken, rice, and buttermilk biscuits, Freeman sits at the kitchen table and feels the familiar jones coming down. Time to go and hit up before the shakes start, then the sweats, then the chills and cramps, yeah, definitely time to hit up. His grandmother interrupts his thoughts.

"Baby, come with me, I got somethin' for you."

Freeman rises from his place at the table and follows his grandmother into the living room. Miss Mable gets down on her hands and knees and rolls back the rug that is carpeting the floor. Underneath it he sees a stack of bills that his grandmother takes into her hands. She rises up and presents it to him. "This is for you baby, I saved it for you all this time."

"Where'd you get that, grandma?" Freeman says as he stares down at the money his grandmother has forced into his hands.

"Why, baby, that's what you sent me when you were over there."

"Grandma, that was for you."

"No, baby, I don't need it none, I saved it for you baby, for when you come home."

Jeremy tries to give the money back, but his grandmother refuses to accept it.

"Get your purse, grandma, we're going to town. Where's the keys to Cousin Rory's car out front?"

"Hangin' by the back door where they always been."

Freeman takes his grandmother's hand and leads her out front. Upon arriving on Renault's Main Street, Freeman leads her into Miss Maryann Dent's beauty shop. "Is it really the Freeman boy?" Miss Maryann exclaims.

"Miss Maryann, I want you to fix my grandma up so she looks real pretty. I want you to fix her hair and put some of that makeup on her face."

Freeman sits down and watches the transformation.

They head over to the Hortense and Hortense Department Store. "Do you like that dress in the window, grandma?" Freeman points.

"Baby, that costs too much."

Freeman grabs his grandma's hand and takes her inside.

The eager clerk rushes over to Miss Mable and asks her what size she would like the dress in.

"I don't quite know son, I never bought me no dress at no store before."

The clerk guesses at the size and returns with the dress.

"Where can my grandmother try that on?" Freeman asks.

"Right this way, ma'am."

Mable comes out in the navy blue, white polka dotted dress, blushing because of the low cut lace collar.

"That fits you just beautiful, ma'am," the clerk says, and looks at Freeman for his approval.

Freeman grabs his grandmother's hand and takes her over to the shoe section. He picks out a pretty pair of navy blue pumps and the clerk rushes over to secure the right size. Freeman states, "Bring my grandmother some of those stockings and whatever else she'll need to go along with them."

Freeman grabs her hand again and takes her over to where the televisions and other major household appliances are located. The clerk is right behind them.

Freeman addresses the man, "I want you to get the biggest and best color TV you got here and load it in the car out front. Then, I want you to deliver one of these washers and one of those dryers to the Edwards' place."

"Yes, sir."

Mable interjects, "Baby, that costs too much."

"Be quiet, grandma." Freeman looks down at her and smiles, the first smile since he's been back to the States.

He follows the clerk up to the cash register and pays his tab in full with the cash his grandma had stashed for him under the rug, and adding a bit more from the wad he has in his uniform pocket.

On the way out of Hortense and Hortense, Mable passes by a full-length mirror and stops to stare. She hardly recognizes herself. "You look beautiful, grandma," Freeman says and bends down to kiss her on the cheek. She looks up into his eyes, saddens again because of their blankness, and tries to smile.

Rory walks through the back door of his home and wonders why his wife isn't in the kitchen to greet him. She is usually there by the stove when he comes in from his day's work.

"Miss Mable?"

Instead of his wife coming around the corner into

the kitchen to greet him, his grandson, his grandson who he never thought he'd ever see again, walks in and stands there staring into his eyes.

"Son, is that you?"

"It's me, Cousin Rory."

For the second time in his life, Freeman is given a quick embrace by his grandfather. Rory quickly surveys his grandson, sees the change that has occurred, and wonders how he is going to tell the boy about his daddy. He decides to wait, he thinks that he might as well let the boy enjoy his first day home.

"Where's Miss Mable?"

"She's out on the front porch."

Rory peers out onto the porch through the screen door. Mable is sitting there on the swing rocking gently and blushing furiously. Rory gives her the once over, shakes his head in confusion, and turns back to Freeman.

"Son, there's a fancy woman on the porch but I don't see Miss Mable."

Freeman realizes that his grandfather is not joking.

"Cousin Rory, that is Miss Mable," he says, working hard to keep a straight face.

Rory steps out onto the porch. He addresses his wife hesitantly, "Miss Mable, is that you?"

Freeman watches through the door.

Shyly Miss Mable nods her head in answer to her husband's question. He looks down at her ankle, where the slave bracelet Miss Mable received from her mother made out of dimes and nickels should be, and he sees the bracelet right where it's always been.

Rory says, "Miss Mable, you're a fine figure of a woman."

He joins his wife on the swing and they rock in unison. Freeman turns and heads for his bedroom. He is pleased that his grandparents are getting pleasure out of something so simple. Now that he has accomplished what he had been wanting to do for his grandmother all his life, the bubble bursts and Freeman wants to be alone. The warmth emanating from that porch is suddenly too much for him to endure.

As he lies there on his bed with his fingers laced behind his head, he sees his grandfather enter the bathroom directly across the hall. Rory sharpens his straight razor on the strap that is hanging there from the wall, lathers up, and scrapes the gray stubble off his face and neck. Then he opens the medicine chest and splashes rubbing alcohol on his chin, cheeks, and neck, the only type of after shave he's ever known. Rory closes the door then, and Freeman hears the water running to fill the bath. Rory's getting all spruced up, and it's not even "Friday e'en," as he would say.

Freeman smiles for a moment. But the smile evaporates as he sees the shadows alter and shift inside his room. He gets up slowly and closes the door. Freeman pulls out his syringe and opium. He sits on the edge of his bed pushing down the plunger, pulling it back slowly until the plastic tube fills with his blood, and pushing it down again slowly, again and again.

aaaahhh what a rush

Freeman closes his eyes in pleasure, the hypodermic still dangling from his arm. After sitting still, enjoying the drug's power, he removes the equipment from his vein and hides it beneath the dresser, right next to where he retapes his supply of opium.

He lies back down on the bed in the darkness and tries to block out the noises inside his head. Every time he closes his eyes he sees tracers, hot and white, zipping back and forth over his eyelids. He is afraid to go to sleep... the dreams will come again and Doc will die. As Freeman lies there thinking of all his friends who died and the friends that he left behind, he knows that he, too, should be dead. He wishes that he was dead.

Freeman lies in the bed of his youth, wondering about his future. His eyes are open searching the night, his ears perk listening for distant chunks of mortar expended into the perimeter, and the pop pop pop of automatic weapon fire. Suddenly, like a marionette, he swings his legs around and sits on the edge of the bed, his feet smooth against the floorboards. He sits there in the night silence, listening. He feels a nakedness and a stabbing need to be out of the confines of his room.

He rises and slides on a pair of green army fatigues and, after buttoning them, grasps his dogtags around his neck as they clink together.

Freeman walks slowly into the living room where

Rory's .22 is hanging on the wall over the fireplace, the same rifle he went hunting with when he was a boy. He gently removes the weapon, grabs the box of shells nearby, and walks soundlessly to the front door. He opens it, and steps outside into the night. He makes his way over and towards the woods and steps into their blackness.

Freeman's eyes and ears are alert as he makes his way through the dense growth. He watches the shadows all around, the weapon cradled in his arms with his finger on the trigger ready to depress. He crouches and begins to run through the foliage toward the river in the distance.

Upon reaching the river Freeman finds a secluded grotto and positions himself inside it so he can see any activity in the woods around him. He lies on his belly with the weapon's butt against his shoulder, ready to fire. For the first time since leaving Nam he feels fully alive. His bare feet are scraped, cut, and bleeding. His arms and chest are scratched from the branches that whipped across them on his night time journey. Freeman doesn't notice the pain.

The nature sounds around him begin to lull him, and as they become louder in his ears Freeman relaxes and drifts off to sleep.

Freeman awakens abruptly. He sits quickly and surveys the area around him. "Where are my men?" he thinks, then remembers that he is not in Nam but at home, out in back of the house in the woods.

He rises and walks to the river, lays down his weapon and drinks deeply from his cupped hands. He splashes water on his face, neck, and chest, shaking the residue by violently jerking his head back and forth. He picks up the weapon and sits on the bank, cradling it across his lap. Freeman feels inside the large pocket of his fatigues and feels the extra shells he had put there the night before. He brings the weapon up and begins to fire at foliage along the opposite bank of the river. Green shoots break in half and fall to the ground.

When Freeman has expended all the rounds, he rises and makes his way to his Secret Place on the hill. From there, he looks down on the surrounding farms that are tinted heliotrope just before sunrise. His loneliness and confusion bring on the hollow death feeling once again. He sits there and weeps. As the light turns from purple to pink, Freeman makes his way back to the house where the needle and opium wait for him.

Freeman sits on the bed in his stuffy room watching the slow infusion of light into the fading darkness. Soon after his return he had heard his grandmother make her way past his room to the kitchen to begin her day's work. The smells of freshly brewed coffee and baking biscuits fill his bedroom. He looks down at the watch on his arm and sees that it is 0530 hours.

He is barefoot and bare-chested, still wearing the fatigues that he had put on earlier in the night. His elbows and forearms rest on his thighs, his hands are clasped together between his knees. He sits staring down at the floorboards, feeling a deeper confusion and aloneness than he ever felt in his life. "No one would understand what it was like," he thinks to himself, "no one."

Once again, the room becomes too much for him to endure. Freeman pulls the bedroom door open and pads softly down the hall. When he walks into the kitchen he stands staring at his grandmother's back, she is unaware of his presence. When she turns around she sees Freeman and is startled.

"Baby, you still sneak up on folks like you use to when you was a boy."

She tries to laugh to ease her nerves. Her grandson just stands there looking ahead at her, looking right through her.

She can't help but notice the long jagged scar running across his belly and tears cloud her eyes. Mable turns around quickly so Freeman won't see them.

"Sit down, baby, breakfast will be ready in just a little while. Your Cousin Rory will be down soon."

Without responding, he moves over to the table and sits down. He hears Rory's field boots coming down the stairs.

"Mornin', Miss Mable."

"Mornin', Mr. Rory."

"Mornin', son."

"Mornin', sir."

"Do you want some coffee, baby?" she says to Freeman.

"Yeah, thanks."

Freeman sits there just staring down at his plate. Mable brings over three ceramic cups of steaming coffee and joins the two men at the table.

Rory speaks, "Son, Miss Mable and I thought it would be best if we waited till today before tellin' you this. Your daddy died when you were over there." Rory continues to cradle the coffee cup in his large, scarred hands and stares down into its ebony pool, not knowing what else to say.

Freeman utters one word, "How?"

Rory raises his eyes to meet his grandson's. "He was down in that Florida, that's all we know 'bout it. Vera got one of them mailgrams one day sayin' that your daddy was dead, that's all we know."

Freeman looks down at his plate and mutters under his breath, "I could have come home."

He gets up slowly and walks out of the kitchen without saying another thing.

Rory and Mable sit at the kitchen table in silence looking at each other for the answers to the many questions they have inside their heads, but neither knows even how to formulate the questions.

After seeing her husband off to the field, Mable makes her way down the hall with a plate full of food. "I got to get the boy to eat," she thinks.

At his bedroom door she stands listening. There is no sound coming from inside, no sobbing, no sound whatsoever. Her hand, reaching out to grab onto the door knob, is shaking. She opens the door slowly.

When the door opens she sees Freeman sitting on the edge of the bed pumping the plunger up and down, his eyes closed. The sound of the door opening makes him look up. He sees his grandmother standing there inside the threshold staring at his arm.

"Baby, what's that you're doin'?"

"It feels good, grandma."

"Baby, are you a doctor?"

"It feels good, grandma, that's all."

"But you're still not a doctor, baby."

Freeman removes the needle from his arm and places it on the bed next to his thigh out of his grandmother's sight. "I'll be right out, grandma. I'm okay now."

"But you're still not a doctor, baby."

Miss Mable turns, leaves the room and returns to her kitchen. Freeman sees the intense pain in her eyes.

He sits there on the edge of the bed as a deep and

excruciating shame envelopes him, a shame that over-shadows the power of the opium in his veins. The one thing in the world that he did not want to do was hurt the woman who just left his room. His tears of shame are mixed with tears for the loss of his father.

Freeman looks for his assignment on the duty roster and sees that he will be responsible for survival training, ranger training, taking the men out, and making them hump. Freeman smiles and heads over to meet his men.

They line up without being told. Having already completed Basic and AIT they know what is expected of them. Freeman is not impressed. He walks slowly up and down the line of men and stares each man in the face as he passes him.

Freeman stops, steps back a few paces, and begins to speak softly, "If you green-ass maggots want to survive in Nam you better listen to everything I have to say. This is your last chance before you get in the jungle and hump and have the fuckin' dinks shootin' at your asses. I want you maggots to get your sorry asses back to your barracks, load your rucks with what you will need to survive, and report back here with your weapons, ASAP, if not sooner."

His voice suddenly booms and gets louder, "I mean *now*, maggots, goddamn it, move!"

The men break and run like they are told. They return and line back up, their chests heaving and sweat running down their faces. Freeman gives them the order to unpack their rucks and lay the contents out before them on the ground. He wants to see what each man has packed for his six-week stay in the bush.

When Freeman sees the lack of preparedness he flies into a tirade.

"All you maggots are going to die! Charlie gonna get your ass pinned in the goddamn bush and you'll run out of ammo and the dinks will systematically pick you apart! Where's your goddamn ammo, man? You stupid motherfuckers carryin' too much bullshit. I want you to shitcan all that bullshit and repack your rucks with fuckin' ammo! You won't last five minutes in Nam! If I was depending on you maggots I'd blow your sorry asses away my goddamn self, save the dinks the goddamn job."

Freeman shoves the man closest to him and the force of it makes him land hard on his ass. He sits there looking up at Freeman, filled with hatred. Freeman stares

140

back and sees the fallen man's displeasure.

"You got a problem with something, shit for brains?"

"Yes, Sergeant!"

"Is it something I can help you with?"

"Yes, Sergeant!"

"Well, what is it, you simple son of a bitch?"

The other men are standing at attention and trying to side-glance the situation. All of them are hoping that their comrade will flatten this sucker on his ass. The fallen man, Christopher Evans, is a big honky who never liked niggers any way, and having one train him and push him around is more than he can stand.

"I don't like your attitude, Sergeant!" the man screams militarily.

Freeman places his foot against the man's shoulder and pushes, "Well, pick your sorry ass up and do something about it, maggot!"

Evans bolts up and rushes Freeman, grabs him around the waist and uses his head as a battering ram in Freeman's belly. Freeman grabs him by the ears and smashes his face down on his knee while bringing his knee up hard. Evans falls to the ground, blood flowing from his mouth.

"You're dead, asshole!" If you grab Charlie like that

in a hand-to-hand combat situation the motherfucker will kill you. When you hit a motherfucker, man, you kill him. Wrestling won't get it in Nam, it ain't the motherfuckin' gym."

Freeman turns and faces the other men, "Do I make myself clear to all you maggots?"

The men cry out, "Yes, Sergeant!"

"I want you Barbie Dolls to strap your rucks to your backs and follow me, I'm gonna teach you sorry assholes how to hump." Freeman smiles then takes off running.

The men grunt and shoulder their loads and follow Freeman as he leads them back into the woods. The shrubs and trees inside the woods are dense, deer flies snap at the men making them wince with their sting. Freeman sees one man, Dempsey, slap at his neck and holler out at the pain. Freeman stops dead in his tracks.

"Come here, troop."

Dempsey runs toward the front of the line of men and stands at attention in front of Freeman. "Yes, Sergeant!

"Do you, maggot, know how far a scream carries in the motherfuckin' bush?"

"Bush" cascades up and out of Freeman's belly like an explosion of dynamite.

"No, Sergeant!"

"You just got half your squad wiped out, you sorry son of a bitch. You deal with the fuckers next time man, the skeeters in Nam are twice as bad, you better get use to the shit."

After four hours of humping at an accelerated pace, a man faints with exhaustion. Freeman comments, "That maggot just got himself killed and the three motherfuckers humping with him. You have to be alert at all times."

He addresses the man appointed as his RTO, "Call in for a medevac to pick up that worthless lump of shit. I want him the fuck out of ranger training, send him back to beauty school."

Freeman turns and starts to pick up the pace again. His radio man calls back for the chopper and the other men try to keep up with their leader's pace. They all start to realize that Freeman knows what he's talking about, it starts to sink in that he has been where they are going and that he has survived.

After hours of constant pounding through the bush, Freeman orders his men to remove their entrenching tools from their rucks and dig. Fill up the sandbags, set the trips up around the perimeter, and go on three-hour shifts of watch with your trench-mate. Ambush.

Freeman lies there in his trench with his RTO and drifts off to sleep. He is back in Nam... he sees the mortar round come and blast into Doc's chest... he sees Doc's head fly away and Doc's blood spurting out of the stump that used to be his neck… he sees Sonny's head roll on the ground… he sees Mehall's stumps protruding out of his fatigues… he sees Gray's chest dripping blood and the rise, fall, shudder, and eventual stilling… he sees Lockhart with his head cradled between his hands shaking his head in disbelief… he sees a gook standing above him with his bayonetted weapon getting ready to thrust it into his belly… Freeman wants to scream and wake up, the gook's weapon is poised and in slow motion it is coming down to hit his vitals… he is exiting the aircraft, he feels the hot lead enter his belly and rip his thumb away from his hand… Freeman wakes up.

Covered with sweat he sits there in the trench and hyperventilates. His RTO asks, "Are you okay Sarge?"

"Yeah, I'm okay."

Freeman lies back down and covers his face with his arm, his elbow sticking up right over his eyes.

doc goddamn it man goddamn goddamn it

After their six weeks in the field, the men have developed new feeling for Freeman. They all want to ask him questions about Nam, but something in Freeman's attitude makes them hold back.

Freeman is glad that they refrain from questioning him, he wouldn't know how to verbalize what happened over there anyway.

Freeman is resting one evening after training when two armed MP's come into his barracks and demand that he accompany them to see the major in charge of the rangers at Benning.

The two MP's lead Freeman silently to personnel. The only sounds are the distant echoes of drill and cadence, and the weapons fire coming from the target range, which disturbs Freeman and makes him feel nervous. Freeman, walking between the two MP's who are looking ahead of themselves without a thing to say, feels like a prisoner. He is.

They reach the drab brick building that serves as the headquarters for the rangers at Benning. One MP opens the door and follows the other MP and their prisoner inside after they step past him. The sergeant at the typewriter looks up. "Major Howard is waiting," he says.

The MP who seems to be in charge walks over to the shut door and knocks.

The MP waiting with Freeman in the background grips Freeman's arm and ushers him toward the door. The MP who knocked holds the door open for them to enter, staring ahead at the wall.

Freeman is led by his escort into Major Howard's office. Both men walk to the front of Major Howard's desk, salute smartly, and stand at attention, waiting for the command.

Major Howard stands and takes his time staring into each man's face. Both men remain silent and erect with respect.

Before leaving his barracks, Freeman had donned his dress uniform: his paratrooper boots, pants tucked inside them below the knee, shirt pressed and tucked into the waistband, on the top of his head the black beret that only airborne rangers can wear, and over his shirt the green jacket that holds all the insignias that tell who he is and what he's done:

Vietnam Service Medal with Three Bronze Stars; two Overseas Bars; Vietnam Campaign Medal with 1960 Device; Combat Infantryman Badge (1st Award); National Defense Service Medal; Purple Heart;

Parachutist Wings with thirty-eight jump insignias; three Weapons Badges: Sharpshooter (M-16); Marksman (M-16); Expert (M-14, M-16, M-60); and his nameplate on his chest; the blue patch of the 173rd Airborne Brigade with a white eagle's wing and red sword on the left sleeve of his jacket, his sergeant stripes on the right sleeve.

Major Howard addresses the waiting MP, "You can leave, wait outside."

The man salutes, "Yes, Sir!"

Major Howard sits down and stares up at Freeman, who is looking at the American flag hanging on the wall behind the Major's desk.

Major Howard leans back. "At ease, Freeman," he says.

Freeman relaxes, spreads his feet apart in the at ease position, and clasps his hands loosely behind his back. He looks down at Howard.

There is a chair right next to Freeman, and Howard says, "Sit down, soldier."

Freeman obeys.

Howard looks at Freeman and begins to speak, "Freeman, do you know why you are here?"

"No, Sir."

"You're here because the FBI intercepted some marijuana that you were shipping back to the States from Nam."

Freeman doesn't respond.

Howard continues, "They intercepted it at the airport and traced it back to you through the address it was to be delivered to in Renault, Mississippi, the addressee was a Miss Mable Edwards. Upon questioning her they knew she had no knowledge of this and ascertained that you were the responsible party."

Freeman doesn't respond.

"Do you have any response to this, Freeman?"

"No, Sir."

"Then you admit that this is true?"

"Yes, Sir."

"I'm afraid that I have no alternative then but to release you into the custody of federal officers. You will be tried and judged in a court of law. Not a military court, a criminal court of law."

Freeman doesn't respond.

Howard picks up the phone and speaks, "Send them in."

Two plain clothes federal agents enter and request Freeman to stand. They grab his arm and force it behind his back and slip a cuff onto his wrist.

Howard says, with suppressed rage, "Is that really necessary, gentlemen?"

"It's procedure, Major Howard."

148

Freeman's other hand is dragged behind his back and the cuff is clicked tightly into place.

They escort Freeman outside and the soldiers in the outer office stare. Freeman feels no fear, he's faced things darker and much more frightening than this.

Freeman spends three days in a cell before his appointed time to come before the judge who will try him for the felony offense he has committed. There are no thoughts inside his head, he spends his days doing push-ups or staring at the wall across from the bunk he sits on, or sitting there with his forearms resting on his thighs, his hands clasped in front of his knees.

His court day comes and Freeman is escorted in front of the presiding judge who will hear his case. Freeman is dressed, once again, in his uniform.

He stands at attention and looks straight ahead and into the eyes of the judge. Judge Campbell breaks eye contact first by looking down at the sheaf of papers before him. He ruffles through the papers and begins to read. When satisfied, he looks ahead at Freeman.

"Sergeant Jeremy Freeman?"

"Yes, Sir."

"Do you understand the charges that have been brought against you?"

"Yes, Sir."

Judge Campbell asks, "Do you have an attorney, young man?"

"No, Sir."

He continues, "Were you read your rights, Sergeant Freeman?"

"Yes, Sir."

"Did you understand your rights, Sergeant Freeman?"

"Yes, Sir."

"Did you understand that if you could not afford an attorney that one would be appointed to defend you free of charge?"

"Yes, Sir."

"Are you prepared to defend yourself against these charges?"

"Yes, Sir."

Judge Campbell starts his questioning. "Did you, Sergeant Freeman, with the knowledge that it was illegal to do so, arrange to have marijuana transported back into the United States from Vietnam?"

"Yes, Sir."

"You admit your guilt in this felony action, Sergeant Freeman?"

"Yes, Sir."

Judge Campbell looks down at Freeman. "Perhaps, Sergeant Freeman, you would like to say something in your defense before I pass judgment on your case?"

"Yes, Sir."

"Go ahead, son."

"Sir, I had no intention of selling any of the marijuana. I was wounded when I was over in Nam and I have a lot of pain because of the wounds. I had a bad opium habit when I came back to the States and I kicked it myself, but the pain is still there, Sir, and I needed something to help it go away."

After looking at Freeman, whose eyes are unwavering, Judge Campbell says to Freeman, "Sergeant Freeman, I have no choice but to render the following decision. Do you, Sergeant Freeman, have any further intentions of attempting to smuggle illicit contraband into the United States?"

"No, Sir."

"Then I render this decision." Judge Campbell looks at the two arresting officers, the prosecuting attorney, the court reporter, the armed officer who escorted Freeman into his courtroom and, finally, at Freeman. "Case dismissed."

He pounds his gavel.

Freeman says, "Thank you, Sir."

Freeman is surprised when he walks into the men's barracks and hears his men greet him with cries of "WELCOME BACK SARGE!"

They are all standing at attention in front of their bunks waiting for his inspection. They face straight ahead, but their eyes are rolled over towards the side of their heads so they can take in Freeman's reaction.

Freeman tries his best to hide his smile, but a little glimmer of it turns his mouth up at the corners regardless. The men see this and are glad, maybe the Sarge will be a little easier on them today.

Freeman walks up and down the line of men

looking each man in the eyes as he passes him. When he has made his way up and down the gauntlet of troops, he stands at the front of the line, right in the middle of the floor, and addresses them.

"If you maggots think that I'm going to be easier on you for this you're dead wrong. I'm going to be harder on you now because I like you sons of bitches. Ain't you lucky?"

The men cry out, "Yes, Sergeant!"

"You maggots got exactly five minutes to report to me on the perimeter of the parade ground with your rucks loaded and your weapons."

Freeman turns and hears the noise behind him of the men preparing themselves for their hump. When he gets to the door of the barracks he stops and turns around, "Hey, you maggots!"

The men drop what they are doing and stand at attention.

"Thanks." Freeman laughs, turns around, and exits the barracks. He hears the men getting ready as he walks away from the long building.

And so it goes for Freeman, month after month, as he trains one batch of new men after another, gives them the best chance he can to get out alive, then sees them off to Vietnam. It becomes just a job, and the job wears on him. His old wounds, his memories hurt. He's in no shape to go back to Nam, back into action. When his hitch is over, Freeman doesn't sign up again. He packs his belongings and takes a bus to Renault, Mississippi.

He spends very little time with his grandparents. Cousin Rory has taken ill, the first time in his life, and at the hospital he is diagnosed as having had a massive stroke. Freeman visits him and kisses the old man on the forehead. His two brothers and Uncle Hank are with him, Freeman holds the old man's hand while he dies. The four men return to Miss Mable's place. Geri and her husband, Geoffrey, will soon sell their house and move in with Miss Mable. Not too much later, Miss Mable will just pine away. The only thing she will want and continually request is "to see that big black man walk through this door."

After Rory's funeral, Freeman decides to return to Chicago with his two brothers and Uncle Hank. Uncle Hank has a spare room and Freeman needs a change. This little pissant town holds too many memories for him, and opportunities in Renault are limited. Freeman packs up again, and rides back to Chicago with the other men.

Freeman likes the feel of his full length gray and burgundy leather coat. It has huge side pockets he can bury his hands in and its tail floats out behind him. The leather is soft and supple, thanks to the generous amount of mink oil Freeman has spent hours rubbing into its surface. More than anything, however, Freeman likes the rich animal leather smell that floats around him. He is working full time in a factory and the coat is his first purchase to stave off the chilliness of Chicago's autumn season.

It's Sunday morning. Knowing that you can't buy beer until noon, and seeing that old man Hank has only a half a bottle of J&B in the house, Freeman picks up the phone and dials his brother Davie.

"You got any beer, shithead?"

"Yeah, I'm sleepin' man, why the hell you callin' so goddamn early?"

"I'm sick, man. I'm comin' over, meet me downstairs."

"Yeah, all right."

Freeman steps out of his car in front of the Robert Taylor Homes, the projects where Davie, his wife Betty, and his daughter Tammy live.

Walking up the gravel path Freeman is greeted by graffiti on sand colored wall. As he nears the building he sees his brother step out of the shadows to greet him. They nod to each other and begin walking side by side to the elevator bank. Silence is their companion.

The reek of urine is the pervading aroma around the outside elevator bank. Davie punches the call button and he and Freeman hear the gears clank and the motor start.

The elevator makes it to the ground floor. Freeman and Davie step in and Davie presses the number fourteen button to take them to his apartment. Davie's hands are visiting the front pockets of his jeans, he is coatless and has no socks. His brother is wearing black dress pants with black Florsheim boots, a white and black patterned silk V-neck dashiki, and his leather coat. Freeman looks overly prosperous in these surroundings.

At the fifth floor the elevator comes to a jerky stop. The door opens and a man steps on. He moves toward the back of the car next to Freeman. His eyes are nearly bugged out of his head as he takes in Freeman's attire. Suddenly, without warning, the man is holding a snub-nosed .32 to Freeman's temple.

Shaking with fear, he blurts out, "Give me the motherfuckin' coat."

Freeman turns his head slowly, the barrel of the gun still insistent against his temple, and confronts the man with his eyes, "I ain't givin' you a motherfuckin' thing," he responds coldly.

Forgotten in the other corner Davie says, "Jeremy, give 'im the coat."

Freeman ignores the metal against his temple and the man holding it, "I ain't givin' him a motherfuckin' thing."

Sweat breaks out on Davie's forehead. "Give 'im the motherfuckin' coat, Jeremy," he says.

Freeman repeats, "I ain't givin' him a motherfuckin' thing."

The junkie starts hopping from one foot to the other like he has to piss. "If you don't give me the coat man, I'm gonna blow your fuckin' brains out!"

Freeman faces him once again. "Go ahead mother-fucker, there'll be blood and brains all over and it won't be worth a motherfuck to nobody."

The elevator door opens on the eleventh floor, no one is there. The man hops outside, the .32 still grasped in his hand. As the door begins to close he addresses Freeman, "You're crazy, man, you're crazy."

Davie, standing in the corner opposite his brother, looks hard at Freeman and believes that what the man just said might be true.

I was nothing when I met Freeman. I was a totally ignorant nineteen year old who thought she knew everything. I had a very low opinion of myself and hadn't learned that I was a person worth loving. I damn sure didn't love myself. I lied to myself constantly and to all the people around me, I felt that these stories and images of myself that I was trying to create would make people love me and respect me. I wasn't being myself.

I had just left my husband of one year, a marriage that was ill-fated from the beginning. He and I had met in a drug abuse program, and I believe that I was using him, and him me, as a replacement for the support that we received there.

Since Danny is black and I am white, people tried to dissuade me from developing the relationship that I was forming with him. I was still in the program, in what they called "second phase," where you live in but go out into the community and establish a place for yourself in society, and I was attending high school with the hopes of obtaining my diploma. Danny, who was in "third phase," where you live out but report back periodically, and I were the topic of many second phase meetings where my peers would ask me why I wanted to associate with a man who seemed to play around so much. They also pointed out to me that I was destined for a really heart-breaking experience.

Because I was so impressionable, instead of telling them to mind their own goddamn business, I listened to them and they successfully planted a seed of doubt in my mind that I, in turn, nurtured and fertilized until it blossomed.

I was very surprised, not too much later, when I was nominated for graduate status. All I had to do was make it through the one-on-one interview with the program director, who came all the way from New York to test the nominees. I did, and at the conclusion of the interview he said, "Congratulations, graduate!"

I had been in the program since age fifteen and at seventeen I had finally finished something. I had started many things before that in my short life, but this was the first time I had ever completed something that I had started.

I moved out of the program facility and in with two other ladies who were graduates of the program. The first day I was free, I had someone buy me a bottle of booze and I got plastered. The seed that was planted in my head before was in full bloom, enhanced by my first experience with alcohol in over two years.

Although Danny and I had no formal commitment then, I knew he was planning to ask me to marry him. All of my girlfriends tried avidly to convince me not to get more deeply involved with Danny, I think now due to jealousy at their not having steady relationships.

When one of them even confessed to having had sex with Danny in the not too distant past, the tender leaflet of courage in me shot up and became a strong tree. I decided to get back at Danny in the only way I knew. I went to bed with someone, lay there feeling lousy, and called Danny the next morning to tell him that I wanted to break off our relationship. I even confessed my deed to him to help him along. His reaction took me by complete surprise, he choked out his intention of marriage. I then told him my reason for not wanting to continue our relationship and he told me that what had happened between him and my roommate had happened many months ago. I told him that it hurt like yesterday.

There was no trust in my relationship with Danny and there never would be. It ended about a year later and I moved in with a married couple to whom Danny, oddly enough, had introduced me. They had a young child and I became a live-in nanny while not at work myself. I was living on Chicago's South Side now, full of fear at the reality that I was alone, and had my second full-time job in the city. I had been promoted twice on my first, and once on the job I currently had. I just couldn't see the gift I had, a gift of being a person who could teach herself things and catch on very quickly.

I was earning enough money now finally to be able to get an apartment of my own. Although the thought terrified me, it also filled me with excitement. I would discover for the first time in my life true independence. There was this old rebel inside of me that had yearned for freedom — by age twelve I was doing any type of drug, sleeping around, drinking, and even attempting suicide at fifteen. Now it was elated at the prospect of finally having it.

I had a girlfriend at work who shared the same taste in men that I have. I wasn't attracted to men of my own race at all, the men who caught my eye were always of the darker complexion.

My girlfriend Nancy and I had been associating with each other for quite a while, going down and having beers on our lunch hours, and we started to become what I thought was very close. She offered to introduce me to the landlord in the building where she lived on Sheridan Road on the North Side of Chicago, a big step up for me.

It all worked out fine and it seemed so much easier than I had ever thought it would be. I signed my lease for my little studio, a furnished apartment, went to the corner grocery store and bought myself some food and beer and decided to have my very own little housewarming party. The unreality of my freedom was leaving me confused and numb.

Every morning Nancy and I would meet down in the lobby of our building and ride the bus to work together. We'd have a few drinks together after work, then she would go home to her two dogs and wait for her lover, and I'd go home to my little nest and become restless and lonely.

One Saturday morning I was watching television when someone knocked on my door. I got up and looked out the peephole, it was Nancy.

I opened the door and let her in.

"Hey Samantha, I was going to go up on Broadway to the record store and see if they have this album Manny said he wanted. Want to come along?" (Manny was her black lover).

Elated at the prospect of not having to be alone any longer, I readily agreed.

"Nancy, I have some beers in the box, go ahead and have one while I get ready. Grab me one while you're at it."

We walked up on Broadway, found the album that Manny had mentioned on his last visit, and decided that we'd stop in a bar and have another beer. It was, after all, a three-day weekend, Labor Day weekend, and we had three whole lovely days to party. We sat there together in a booth in a darkly lit bar and talked with each other about things that I can't even remember. On our third beer, two black men sauntered over and asked us if they could join us. I was willing, Nancy was a little hesitant, Manny on her mind. The men made up their minds about who was for whom, and the respective man joined the lady he desired on her side of the booth. They started buying the drinks and Nancy and I sure weren't complaining. We decided to head to another bar down the street, and that is a decision that changed my life forever.

We had moved to the other bar, all four of us were sitting there on bar stools, and I was getting pretty chummy with the man I was with. For all I knew he could have been Jack the Ripper, but that would never happen to me.

Then he walked in... a deep reddish-brown complexion, huge shoulders making his physique look like an inverted triangle, big brown eyes, big strong-looking hands, a nose that was sharply defined and hooked. The man I was with, my informal date, was forgotten.

There was music playing on the jukebox and I got right up, walked over to him, and asked him if he would dance with me.

He looked at me, a bit surprised, and said "Okay."

He took another pull off the beer he had ordered, slid off the bar stool, and led me over towards where the music was blasting. My recently deserted companion stared. I couldn't have cared less. Nancy and her companion weren't hitting it off that well either, as Manny was on Nancy's mind.

A slow dance came on and he pulled me close to him. The smell coming from him, along with the subtle cologne I picked up around his face and neck, made me not give a damn what anybody else was thinking. All I could think about were those strong arms that were around me, the strong, hard chest that he so arrogantly pressed up against mine. He stepped away from me and looked into my eyes. I could see his desire and I know that he saw the sparks flying from mine.

He said with much confidence, "Let's get out of here."

I was too overcome even to answer him, I just blindly obeyed and allowed him to lead me out of the bar, leaving my companion there fuming, and Nancy wondering why I had deserted her without so much as a word.

We moved to another bar and he ordered us a couple of beers. We sat together over in a corner and he watched me intently. His scrutiny of me made me very nervous and excited me at the same time. I had never had a man look at me that way before. There was something in his eyes that I have never seen in any one else's, I didn't know whether to be afraid of him.

My hand shaking, I reached into my purse to pull out a cigarette and my lighter. When I got one out of the pack and brought it to my lips his hand shot across the table, lighting my cigarette. I couldn't believe it.

"My name's Freeman."

"I'm Samantha."

"Hi, Sam." A big smile spread across his face. I had to answer it.

Freeman kept the beers coming and he sat there and listened to me as I babbled nervously about myself. Freeman didn't have much to say. He suddenly stood and reached his hand out for mine. "Let's go."

Like a trained puppy, I followed him outside. As we walked down the street he pulled me into an alleyway that secluded us from passers-by. He pulled his cigarettes out of the front pocket of his gabardine slacks and carefully took a joint out from between the pack and cellophane. Freeman lit up.

I looked around nervously, paranoid, as he dragged deeply on the smoke. Freeman handed it to me. I took it and inhaled slowly, deeply, held it in, then handed it back. Freeman wet his forefinger and thumb and extinguished the fire on the end, and put the joint right back where he had got it. Now you see it, now you don't.

We moved back onto the street again and started walking north on Broadway towards Belmont Avenue. I kept looking over at him as he held my hand. He was walking erectly, his eyes alert, seeing everything around us.

"Freeman?" I say. He looks over at me.

"What?"

"Will you come home with me?"

"Yeah."

When we reached the corner of Belmont and Broadway I said, "Freeman, do you want to stop at the store here and get some more beer?"

"I don't have any money."

"I'll buy it."

When we walked inside, a couple of young men walked up to him.

"Hey Freeman, what's goin' on man?"

"Nothin'."

The conversation faded away as I made my way to the back of the store to grab a couple of six packs of beer, the kind he had ordered for us in the bar. The reefer was making me paranoid, as it always had before, and I thought to myself that they were questioning him about me. I started to feel like an aardvark, all low to the ground and ugly. I made my way up to the checkout to pay and Freeman was standing there with his arms behind his back waiting for me. When I saw him there I smiled at him and he nodded his head slightly.

I had noticed before that his cigarettes were low so I asked the clerk for a pack of his and a pack of mine. I counted out the money to the girl behind the register.

When I approached Freeman he reached out and took the bag from my arms to carry them in his own. I felt like a schoolgirl the first time a boy offers to carry her books home for her from school, although I had never had that experience myself, I am sure that is how it must feel.

We had only one block east to go to Sheridan before we would reach my apartment. The landlord was in the office when we walked by to the elevator. When the elevator let us off on my floor, I fumbled inside my purse looking for my keys. Freeman stood behind me waiting patiently.

When we walked inside my little studio, I was glad that I had made my bed before Nancy and I had left earlier in the day. There was my little hide-away couch in the single room, two chairs, a dented table with a lamp, and a wall unit that was built in for additional storage. Freeman headed over to my kitchen, which was located right behind my couch against the south wall, and put the beer in the fridge after taking two out of the carton for us. He sat down on the couch and stared at the blank, black-and-white TV screen that was placed in the wall unit.

"Do you want to watch TV?"

"Yeah."

I turned it on for him and walked through the little walk-in closet that led to my bathroom. When I shut the door I looked at myself in the mirror and hoped that Freeman thought I was pretty. I didn't see how he could, I hated myself.

I returned to the living room/kitchen/bedroom all rolled into one, and was once again handed the joint Freeman had relit when I was in the bathroom doubting myself. I joined Freeman on the couch, the springs and lumps of old age uncomfortable on our butts, and smoked the joint until Freeman put it out again.

"That's one-toke smoke, Sam, you better go easy on that shit."

Nervously, I reached out for my beer that Freeman had put on the table, but again his hand shot out and he handed me the green bottle. I drank deeply.

"Do you want to watch something else? Here's the TV Guide."

I sprang up to get it off the chair it was sitting on only four feet away. I handed it to Freeman.

He looked through it and got up and changed to the channel he wanted. There was boxing on and he sat there moving with the motion of the fighters' punches.

I said, "Ali's going to fight soon, do you want to come over and watch it?"

"Yeah." His shoulders kept rolling with the punches being thrown by the boxers on the tube.

"Are you hungry?"

"Not now, later."

His silence, the silence of our new companionship, was making me very nervous. I felt like I had to keep talking.

I kept babbling on about things that I can't even remember this day. I wondered even then how Freeman tolerated me, I was so young.

The boxing match was finally over in the seventh round by a TKO when Freeman turned to me and said, "I could fall in love with you, Sam."

That shut me up, then the kiss he gave me stifled my conversation completely.

We pulled out my little couch and made it into a bed. Freeman got undressed and lay down waiting for me. A long jagged scar was running across his belly and two dark holes were right over his pubic hairs to the left of his navel. There was a peace sign tattooed right over his right tit, all blue against his hairless reddish brown chest. I stared. Freeman stared back.

I removed my clothes, my hands shaking, and

joined Freeman on the bed.

"Freeman, what's your first name?"

"Jeremy."

"Jeremy, what happened to your stomach?"

He turned over on his side, pulled me close to him and said, "Don't mean nothin', little Sam, don't mean nothin'."

He silenced my next question with his tongue and lips.

We lay there against each other breathing deeply, and he held me tightly against his chest. His mouth found my ear and he whispered, "I'm gonna marry you, Sam."

"I love you, Jeremy," I said.

We hugged each other tighter.

Freeman's embrace was suddenly gone, he stood and walked through my little closet to the bathroom. The door shut and I could hear the stream of his urine as it hit the water in the toilet.

I got up and put on a green lace negligee, and when Freeman returned he put his shorts on. I was propped up on my pillow waiting for him to put on the rest of his clothes and leave, but he got back into the bed and put his arm around me. He kissed my shoulder and looked into my eyes.

"Fetch us a beer, Sam."

I obeyed.

I got back into the bed with him and suddenly his hand grabed my left arm. He examined the seven scars that crisscross up and down my arm, the jewelry I wear after my attempt to take my own life with a single-edged razor blade.

He looked at me and the hurt I saw there was more devastating than the question, "Why'd you do that, Sam?"

What can I say, I did it and the person I cared about more than anyone in this world, my grandfather, found me. I felt all my life like I never had anyone, I felt like nobody ever really cared about Sam. My own father took me to court when I was thirteen years old because of my suicidal behavior, and the presiding judge asked him, "Who do you want, your wife or your daughter?" My heart broke when he indicated the former. My parents had been at the end of their ropes, they didn't know what to do with me and thought that the law could help control me. I wasn't ready for help then, that would come later when I volunteered to enter into the drug abuse program.

My real mother had died when I was four years old and my father had remarried. The woman he married is a great woman, but she didn't understand the trauma that I was experiencing because of the loss of my mother. My deceased mother's relatives also added a great deal of pressure to the situation by telling lies to me, like that my father had known and was dating my stepmother prior to my mother's death. Being a young child and so impressionable, I believed them, then questioned my step-mother, didn't believe them any longer until the next time I visited them and they repeated the lies. I was on a merry-go-round of emotional disturbances and fears. This created the monster I became in my youth, a drug-crazed idiot, a confused and frightened little girl.

Be that as it may, I tried to verbalize all of this to Freeman. It came out the best I could get it out, and Freeman held me close to his chest and made love to me.

Tuesday morning rolled around too quickly, I wanted to make these three days with my salvation last forever. When I got dressed to go to work he was still lying there sleeping. I woke him up... so I thought.

The violence in his movement made me fall off the edge of the bed and onto the floor.

"Jeremy!" I screamed out in my surprise.

He looked around himself and made the motion — his hand behind his head in a fist and cocked — to hit me.

His eyes, I will never forget his eyes. Slowly he lowered his hand onto the bed.

His eyes softened and he said, "Where're you goin', Sam?"

"To work," I replied, still fearful of his earlier reaction.

Freeman rose from our bed silently and got dressed while I returned to the bathroom to put on my makeup.

He was sitting on the bed when I returned.

"Will you come over tonight, Jeremy?"

"Yeah. What time?"

"Seven o'clock?" I said, feeling happy about his response but doubtful that he was telling me the truth.

"Okay."

We walked out into the hall together and he put his arm around my waist. I looked up into his face and smiled, Jeremy smiled back. We entered the elevator together and he pushed the button that would take us to the ground floor.

As we disembarked from the elevator, Nancy was waiting there in the lobby for me like she did every other morning that I had been living in the building. She looked at Jeremy, looked but didn't say a thing.

Jeremy turned to me and planted a soft kiss on my mouth. "I'll see you later, Sam."

Nancy and I headed outside to catch the bus on Sheridan Road so we could head down to the Hancock Building where we worked. She was silent all the way there.

It was the longest work day that I could remember. Although I was busy, which would usually make the time fly, the minutes crawled. When 5:00 finally rolled around, I was ready to jump out of the window, if that would get me down to the bus stop any faster. I met Nancy on the way out and she said, "Want to stop in the bar and have a beer?"

I quickly replied, "No, I have to get home."

"Oh, I suppose you're going to see 'him' again?"

I didn't detect the disfavor in her voice. "Yes, he's coming over at 7:00, I want to make sure I'm home."

"Well, I'm going to have a beer. You better take the bus by yourself."

I detected it that time, but I didn't care.

I got on the express bus and it crawled through the Loop in the rush hour traffic. By the time it made its way to the Outer Drive, I was ready to scream. When it turned off on the Belmont exit, I kept glancing at my watch, which read a quarter to six. I kept thinking to myself, "What if he comes over early and I'm not at home?"

When the bus pulled up to the stop on Sheridan, I bolted out of the exit door and waited, impatiently, for the light to change. I crossed the street and waited again for the Belmont light to turn red. It finally did, and I ran across to make my way to the gourmet wine cellar where I purchased some more beer and a package of my brand of cigarettes and a package of his. I ran down the street and rushed through the door of my building.

When I walked into my little studio, the bed was

unmade, just as Freeman and I had left it that morning. I quickly put the beer in the fridge, put the leftover roast in the oven and turned it on low, and finally made up the bed, playing beat the clock all the time. When I looked over at the clock after finishing up my chores, I saw that it was only 6:00. I had an hour to wait.

I paced back and forth. The little confines of my studio and the loneliness I felt were suffocating me. I tried sitting down on the couch and that didn't still the pressure I felt in my heart and chest. I tried lying down and realized that sleep would be the only way that time would pass faster. That was the only way that I could wait for Jeremy and not go insane.

I walked over to the little end table where my windup alarm clock sat ticking, and set it for the alarm to go off at 6:45. I went back to the couch, lay down, and fell into an uneasy sleep.

The clock rang into life at the appointed time, I got up quickly to still the bell and ran into the bathroom to wash my face and re-apply my makeup.

At 7:00, I was sitting there looking at my clock like it was an enemy, my stomach sinking and my heart beating fast. The door buzzer broke the silence of my little room, making me jump.

I opened the door, let him in, and we embraced.

Freeman stayed the night, and the next night, and the next... .

Freeman appointed himself my protector, the only person who ever cared enough to stick by me and help me save my soul. The city jungle is a fierce, wicked place where I never would have survived without him. Sometimes it seemed like the only time he could penetrate my skull was to allow me to fall on my face and let me crack my head. Many times he pushed me down himself, as I had to learn the hard way.

Freeman saw something in me, but I still find it hard to understand why he bothered to take the time. The only conclusion I can reach is that "he saves her to save himself."

Our first four years together are somewhat blurry and distorted in my mind, but the intense clarity of the pain still rings through sharply. Getting to know each other, the sudden mood changes he had, and the violence.

I recall mostly the sort of people he knew and associated with back then. One woman in particular, a hooker hardened by the streets, a woman who told me blatantly that I have no business in this setting, and an older man who was looked upon in the neighborhood as a sort of godfather among the black street people.

I remember when Freeman got himself arrested for drunken and disorderly conduct, and this godfather was the only person I could turn to for the $50 bail I needed to get him out of jail. Walking the Chicago night streets to his apartment five blocks away, I remember only the fear that something would happen to Freeman and that I'd be left all alone.

There were many ladies of the streets vying for his affection; they would even offer him money to pay his rent in the little one room dive he lived in before he deserted his place for mine. He was evicted, really, after I threw an adolescent temper tantrum and smashed my fist through the window.

He would spend many nights walking the streets as I lay there sure that he was with someone else. The other nights when he was gone and I could not bear to lie there all alone, I went out on my own foolish excursions and flirted with the street people up on Broadway, flirting more with death than I realized.

I had no idea or understanding of the reasons for his many hours of silence, no idea that the nightmares I would awaken him from were his living memories, no idea of his pain and anger. He was walking in his dark garden all alone, remembering.

We were living in the little studio apartment I had rented, the confines of the place adding to his feelings of discomfort. When the year was up on my lease, I rented a one bedroom apartment in the same building, which was unfurnished except for a fold out couch the landlord agreed to sell to us, along with two easy chairs, a scratched end table, and a kitchen table with wobbly legs and ripped plastic-covered chairs, all for $100.

After signing the new lease, Freeman and I took our belongings to our new apartment. The living room's paned, one-panel window actually had a view, nothing like the brick wall three feet away from the window that had been our only view in the studio. The kitchen had a window as well, and wasn't dark and confining like the one-room prison we had just left behind.

Actually, the place seemed palatial to us. Freeman and I decided to have a party. It was a good day, and there were many good days to come. There were, however, still times when a dark cloud, ominous and unsettling, would stuff my ears with cotton and loom over my head, when Freeman would disappear without a reason.

He disappeared one day and I decided that I had had enough; I allowed myself to be picked up by three streetwise black guys on the corner where all the homeless, the street people, and the other neighborhood regulars hung out. I took them home and Freeman was there after being gone for at least forty eight hours. I told Freeman my intentions of leaving him while the three black men grabbed our stereo and television. As I stood there looking at Freeman, who was sitting nonchalantly in one of the easy chairs, he said to me, "You're making a big mistake, Sam."

The three men took off into the hallway and headed straight for the elevator. When I finally realized what was happening to me, I ran after them with Freeman following behind me shaking his head in his amazement at my stupidity. I ran out through the lobby and saw the taillights of the car, with the three men inside, taking off onto Sheridan. I had been had.

Freeman was angry, but Freeman stayed. The realization of my own stupidity was an embarrassment so complete that my face and every other part of my being felt scalded. I learned a very valuable lesson that Freeman had been trying to teach me for better than a year: that people would rip me off for anything and everything that I had, even my life if that is how they get their kicks.

Things got so bad for me financially, being in debt over my head for the lost items I literally gave away, that we were barely making it from one paycheck to another, and lived on hard-boiled eggs, toast, and tea for three weeks during one stretch of time. Freeman told me that the only way we could get out of this situation would be for us to move back into the building where he had his little one-room dive when I had met him.

I broke the lease I had at our building, and Freeman and I toted our belongings to his old place. Freeman signed up for and began receiving checks from general assistance, and we stayed there for one year and he helped me pay off the debt I had jumped into and was drowning in. He gave me the opportunity to save up some money and save myself from total ruin. Things started looking pretty good after the debt was gone, and we started looking with longing and desire at the building across the street, what we thought was the nicest apartment complex on Sheridan. We discussed it at length, I had begun to realize that Freeman must always be a part of these decisions, I knew he had more savvy and wisdom than I did, and I sought out his advice before I would commit to anything.

I went over and introduced myself to the landlord one day after work. I was shown a one-bedroom apartment, and signed the lease for our new home. Freeman and I had two months until it would be time to move in, so we headed over to Nelson Brothers and purchased a living room set and bedroom set for our new abode. I had to sign a wage garnishment agreement because of the payment history I had demonstrated with my first defaulted credit card. We saved up enough cash, went down to Polk Brothers and purchased a thirteen-inch color television, a cheap stereo, and a dining-room table.

The two months we waited to move in seemed to the both of us like two years. When the day finally came, we packed our clothes and other belongings for the final time, and made our way across the street to an apartment with a view of the city, a large and spacious living/dining room, a fully equipped kitchen, a large bedroom, nice spacious bath, and wall-to-wall carpeting. We had two weeks to wait for our furniture to be delivered, so Freeman and I slept on the floor in the living room. We didn't care.

When I came home from work the night that the furniture had been delivered, Freeman was not at home to greet me. I was glad in a way that he wasn't, as I wanted all this good fortune I was experiencing to soak in. I needed time alone as I stood there and cried with joy and rubbed my hands lovingly over the furniture Freeman had arranged for me in the living room. That is the first time that I didn't worry about Freeman being somewhere with someone else, I knew right then and there that he loved me and started to realize that there was something unsettling him that was beyond my understanding. I decided to start asking him questions.

As time progressed we grew closer, but the times of his silences were still present and unpredictable in their coming. After three years together he seemed to change suddenly; he began spending more time in our apartment while I was out working at my job in the Loop. I'd come home afterwards just like I always had, but now there would be a light in the living room window welcoming me home. When I walked through the door of our apartment, Freeman would be in the kitchen waiting for me with a smile that hurt my eyes.

The house would be vacuumed and dusted, the laundry he'd done lying on our bed folded and ready to be put away. He'd still take his nightwalks sometimes, but they were growing more infrequent. We'd spend most of our time together in the living room watching television, listening to the stereo, or just talking. He began to tell me of himself in that third year together, things of his childhood, growing up the way he did, what his dreams had been, who his family was.

We grew closer and closer and as his trust and love developed for me into that of a true friend, after four years together, he began to tell me about Vietnam.

I married Vietnam. I married Freeman, Doc, Gonzales, Sonny, Pauly, Mehall, McCall, Jackson, Wilcox, Gray, Colfax, Conner, Johnson… the list goes on and on.

I've watched them die over and over as Freeman relives their deaths with every breath he takes.

It is especially hard for us around holidays, during the Fourth of July when firecrackers are popping all over the neighborhood, it sounds like a fucking war zone out there. It seems as though the people living above us in our apartment building have the fuses timed so the crackers will pop and explode right in front of our window. The first time that happened, nine years ago, Freeman assumed the prone position and reached for his weapon that wasn't there. It made him flip...

Right back into the jungle. I have to keep plenty of Valium around for him because his nerves get so frazzled.

It's devastating for me to sit there and watch him go back to Nam. You'll probably never understand the impact I feel when my heart leaves me and goes back to the jungle, however, I'll try to explain it to you.

We have been experiencing war from the beginning of time, but Nam was different. When the troops came home from Nam they couldn't talk about their war because that isn't what it was, it wasn't a war, according to the popular belief of the age, it was a conflict and the soldiers were "baby killers." So they kept it all inside of themselves and it grew to monstrous proportions.

A conflict is when you and I disagree and mix words airing our differences; a war is when you shoot at people, and they are shooting at you, and people die. Plain and simple. If I must spell it out,

V-I-E-T-N-A-M W-A-S A W-A-R! The longer we deny that the more they will suffer and die.

Our government allowed all the draft dodgers to come home, but ignored the men who fought there. Today, Vietnam is an era dead and gone, while Vietnam vets wonder where all their champions of the past are hiding.

I remember one year during Armed Forces Day, the military was lining up for their annual parade in the vacant parking lot adjacent to the building where I work. I was looking out of the window at them and admiring the men in their uniforms who seemed ready, willing, and able in this peace time to march proudly in the name of militarism, honor, and love of country.

I was openly and frankly proud of them. A female co-worker of mine came up to me and said, "I'd appreciate it if you wouldn't stand here by my cubicle and look at those baby killers, go and do it somewhere else."

I responded, "If it wasn't for those baby killers out there, bitch, you wouldn't be walking around with your delusions and you wouldn't be able to mouth off your insane beliefs in freedom."

Later that day, she bought me a bouquet of daisies. I expect that in her mind that made everything better. All was forgiven. Now the baby killers lie in their beds at night drowning in their memories and nightmares of the abattoir from which they escaped with their lives. It can no longer be an issue as to whether Vietnam was right or wrong, the soldiers who made it back to the World will always remember their fallen comrades, will always weep for them, will always believe that what they died for was a true and just cause. They still, after all of the derision and malice, have love of country and a deep rooted patriotism.

He has hallucinated that I am a gook, and he has come after me with a butcher knife ready to disembowel me. I have never been so afraid of anything in my life. My entire body shook convulsively and my mind was numbed with such a feeling of unreality. I really believed that I was going to die. I lay there on the living room floor, Jeremy was straddled above my body, one knee on each side of my hips, one hand around my throat, the other gripping the butcher knife that glimmered evilly. As I lay there squirming and pleading with him, his eyes changed. As they softened, his hand around my throat loosened and I gasped roughly for some air. When his eyes cleared completely, he threw the butcher knife across the room. Tears were filling his eyes as he pulled me close and held my trembling body. He whispered over and over in my ear, "I'm sorry, Sam, God, please forgive me."

Vietnam veterans hate and do not trust the VA. One day when I was at work, Freeman ran up into a fellow Vietnam vet who had a hairline fracture on his elbow. He told Freeman that when he had gone to the VA they opened his arm up from the shoulder all the way down to his wrist and did their tests. Freeman ran into the guy in a bar, he was sitting there weeping in his beer.

He pulled his sleeve up and showed Freeman the tightly tied, knot sutures. The man was crying because he was unemployed and had no choice but to go back to the VA, he was terrified of what they were going to do to him next.

Freeman told him to stay put and that he'd be right back. Freeman came home and pocketed his surgical scissors and tweezers, he removed a bottle of rubbing alcohol from the medicine chest, bagged it, and made his way back to the bar.

He took 147 tightly tied stitches out of the man's arm. If the procedure had been done correctly, only about ten would have been needed.

This enraged Freeman so much that his eyes changed on me again. There's no half way for a Vietnam veteran, a Lurp, a Grunt, a Ranger. A man who saw frontline combat in the boonies, or as the brothers called it, "Soulville," because of the disproportionate number of brothers, bloods, who died there.

When anything enrages Freeman he flips… there's only one solution that he can arrive at when he is caught inside his anger, "Kill the son of a bitch!" I've lost count of the number of times I've had to restrain him. Once when I called the VA, the counselor I talked to told me to leave Freeman. I asked him if he was married and he told me, "No, my wife divorced me seven years ago."

I told the son of a bitch, "Misery loves company. I bet if you ran up into a sick animal in the gutter that, instead of trying to revive it by taking it home and nursing it back to health, you would probably kick it." A poor analogy, but apt.

Have you ever seen a man kill himself? Ever known a man want to take a weapon and shoot himself in the head? This happened after he received a phone call from a friend telling him that Wilcox, the guy who was over in Nam with him and read the Bible all the time, took a .45 and put it to his temple. He pulled the trigger in front of his wife and three children ranging in ages from four to fifteen.

Freeman asked me what I would do if I came home from work and found him laying there on the floor with a bullet in his head and his brains splattered all over the wall. I told him that I would get a bucket and clean it up, then dress him in his nicest suit, pin his medals on his chest, and try to clean him up the best I could before calling the undertaker. What the fuck did he think I'd do?

The words "hope," "positive," "love," "trust," "God," have little or no meaning to him. The definitions are beyond his comprehension. I, at least, have got him to feeling two of them, the others are still out there some-where waiting to be discovered. But the definitions are still elusive, hidden.

There is a real risk in living with a "grunt." A risk that I have been willing to take because of my love for the man. I've seen him go into malaria flashbacks, I've seen him fall to the floor after his head hits against the sharp edge of the table, and shake convulsively because of the chills that overcome his body. He gets so dizzy that I do not feel secure leaving him home alone. I had to dress him one time, he couldn't even put his own socks on, and take him in a cab to the hospital emergency room. The attending physician loaded him up with Valium and gave me a prescription slip so I could get him some more. I kept him heavily sedated for four days, and even though the drug was in his system he still had the shakes.

He's extremely suspicious when anybody is nice to him. He wonders why. Even when I show him love and understanding he looks at me with a wounding doubt in his eyes.

"If you're lying to me Sam, I'll kill you."

I know he will so I am very careful always to tell him the truth. It got so bad during the Fourth of July, 1987, that I had to take two days off from work and spend hours on the phone with Vietnam veterans at the Vet Center, not affiliated at all with the VA. First I queried them... I asked the vet I was talking to, Charlie was his name, "Are you affiliated at all with the VA?"

Charlie started to laugh and said, "No way, shape, or form. If we were, I goddamn sure wouldn't be here."

"Is there a fee that my husband would have to pay if he came to you guys for help?"

"Lady, if your husband was in Nam, he's already paid his dues."

We talked for hours and I confessed all the things to him that were happening. Charlie made a statement, "Whatever you do, lady, don't let him abuse you. Has he?"

I told him the truth, I told him yes. Many times he's flattened me and come back later to apologize for hurting me. He didn't even remember doing it.

Charlie told me, "If he ever does it again, leave him. You don't deserve that kind of treatment."

He then asked me, "How long have you been married to Freeman?"

"Going on eleven years," I responded.

"You must be a helluva lady," Charlie said.

"Are you married, Charlie?"

"Not any more. My wife left me 'cause she couldn't understand where I was coming from most of the time, she couldn't understand Nam."

"Well, Charlie," I said, "I married Vietnam."

He said, "You got that right."

"Freeman was over there from '67 to '69, he did two tours. He was over there during Tet, he made a combat jump that was ordered by General William C. Westmoreland, he got fucked up during the jump."

Charlie asks, "What was his MOS?"

"11 Bravo, 2 P. Freeman was in Alpha Company, 2nd of the 503rd, 173rd Airborne Brigade."

Charlie says, "Holy Shit! Samantha, I think that the 173rd is having their reunion this weekend right here in Chicago. Let me check my files to see if I have the info. It might take a while, can you wait?"

Elated, I said, "No problem!"

He found it and gave me the name and phone number of the Chicago Chapter president. When Freeman finally came home, he had been walking the streets for the past two days, I told him what I had found out and insisted that he call. I told him that if he didn't I would.

He did. The 173rd Airborne Brigade was meeting right then and there at the Blackstone Hotel on South Michigan Avenue. Freeman identified himself to the Chicago president. The president responded, "You got a way to get down here, man? If you don't we'll send somebody to pick you up."

"I live here in Chicago," Freeman responded, "I'll be over in the morning."

The president made the statement, "Airborne!"

Freeman made the reply, "All the way!"

He was nervous, I've never seen him that nervous. We went up to the corner grocery store together and I cashed him a check for thirty dollars. I told him, before he walked out of the door, "Call me, Freeman."

He stopped, looked at me and smiled, "You call me, Sam, have me paged."

Freeman went to the reunion and the guys there were so organized. There were three men standing there by the reception desk waiting for new guys to arrive, the cherries. Freeman produced his discharge papers and the man pulled information up in the computer telling where the 2nd of the 503rd, 173rd Airborne Brigade was located in the hotel. One of the vets, after being told where Freeman's comrades were, took him into, of course, the bar. Alpha Company, point company, will always be in the bar.

The first man that Freeman made eye contact with was one of the men that had carried him to the medevac when Freeman got shot up. They recognized each other instantly. They made a break across the room and hugged each other, kissed each other's faces, and rolled on the floor together, goosing each other all the time.

I waited that day until about noon, then finally built up enough nerve to call down to the Blackstone Hotel.

"Freeman?"

I hear him answer in the background, "Yeah?"

"Telephone."

"Hello?"

"Hi baby, how are you doing?"

"Sam, thanks, I met a guy, Jackson, who I was over in Nam with. This is unreal, I've taken a lot of pictures, you'll see all the motherfuckers." Freeman laughs.

"You have a real good time there, baby, I'll see you when you get home."

"I love you, Sam."

"I love you too, Jeremy."

When he came home… I've never seen his eyes so happy, they were joyful. The only other time his eyes shone like that was when we went downtown and got married.

"Sky Soldier." He brought home a newsletter of the 173rd. All the things he had told me over the years were verified in its content. Not that I didn't believe him, but it's hard when people tell you that there were no combat jumps made in Vietnam. I would always say to them, "Would you please tell my husband that, maybe the scars will go away."

It hurts me when people tell me that Nam wasn't so bad and that anybody who was there who suffers from PTSD is crazy to begin with. It hurts me because I know what Freeman went through over there, and if the people who are talking all the shit had experienced what he did, they would probably be in a loony bin today, or all tucked away in the VA.

Post-Traumatic Stress Disorder. Freeman was used to surviving in Nam under stressful conditions… he came back to the States and the stress was removed. He some-times goes into places, even yet today, where the element of people there are those who do not like Freeman's race. He will go into those places and be the only black man in there, he's just daring someone to start some shit with him. It is, after all, a free country, a country that he was willing to sacrifice his life for, and he feels that he can go whereever he damn pleases. There's no "white man's door," so far as Freeman is concerned, except for when employment is the issue.

I love when people tell me that he's just lazy and doesn't want to work, I love it because it verifies all the things that people are: ignorant, prejudiced, condescending, arrogant, and just generally walking around with rose-colored glasses on. Walk into any company downtown and count the black executives you see in the office; you will usually find one or two black men in the place, that's all.

Women in the work force say that it's a man's world. Well, that's true to a certain extent, however, they are leaving out a very important adjective in that statement. What they really should say, if they want to be accurate and truthful about it, is "it's a white man's world."

My black man has applied for many jobs, not of the executive nature, but jobs where he can work with his hands and use the many labor skills he possesses. All to no avail.

A couple of years ago, on the way to my parents' home in the suburbs, we passed a factory that had a large sign in front, "positions available." That following Monday morning when I went to work, Freeman went on a mission. He put his nicest suit on, groomed himself so every hair was in place, and drove back out to the factory we had passed on Saturday.

When Freeman entered into the lobby and approached the receptionist, she smiled up at him. He requested an application, she provided one on a clipboard, along with an ink pen, and Freeman sat down on a chair in the waiting room and began filling in the blanks.

Freeman rose and handed the application to the woman behind the desk. He returned to the waiting room, the receptionist picked up her telephone, and minutes later the door behind her opened. A white man took Freeman's application, saying "Mr. Freeman?"

Freeman rose and walked erectly toward the man and the door he was holding open. "Good morning, sir," Freeman reached out his hand, shook the man's, and gave him a smile.

"Good morning. This way please."

Once inside the office, the man offered Freeman some coffee, which he accepted. He began reviewing Freeman's application as Freeman sat on the other side of his desk waiting. When the man got to the end of the application where Freeman had noted his military service, he glanced up nervously at Freeman.

The man saw in Freeman's face dignity and pride. He felt a great welling distaste inside himself, not for Freeman, but at what he had been instructed to do in the event that a situation like this should ever arise. He decided to be honest. Freeman's demeanor dictated the man's reaction. The man looked straight at Freeman.

"Mr. Freeman, I could lose my job for telling you this, but I feel in all fairness that I have to."

"What is it, sir?"

"Mr. Freeman, I've been instructed by the people upstairs to avoid hiring Vietnam veterans who were in combat. I wish I could do something for you, but if I hired you and my boss saw your records, I could lose my job. I'm sorry."

"It has nothin' to do with the fact that I'm black?"

"Not this time, Mr. Freeman. Listen, the only reason that I'm telling you this is that I can see that you are a very respectful man, a very intelligent man. I'm fed up with this shit, but I've got to keep my job, I've got a wife and kids to support, you know?"

"Yeah. Listen, thanks for being honest with me, I won't let it go any further. You could have kept my hopes up, I appreciate you telling me like it is."

Freeman stood, as did the man behind the desk. They shook hands again. "I'm sorry, Mr. Freeman."

"Fuck it, man, don't mean nothin'."

I had no idea that he was going to go and apply for one of those jobs that day. His silence the next three days and his street walking told me that something bad had happened. I waited patiently until the storm raging inside him would ease down to a drizzle. A week later he finally told me.

Fuck it. Don't mean nothin'.

It is something that Freeman and many other vets

who served in heavy combat will have to deal with for the rest of their lives. It is something that they will have to resign themselves to live with.

The malaria flashbacks come and go as they see fit, so does the gout Freeman suffers from lying in muddy foxholes during monsoon season. As does the pain he suffers from his war wounds, the lead still lodged by the nerves in his lower leg sometimes bring about a severe limp because of the pain, and the scar across his belly aches with the rain.

He's wondered many times about what effect Agent Orange will have on him, so I sent him to the hospital for a complete cancer screening. Thank God, everything came up clear, hopefully it will stay that way down the road. The fear remains there inside him all the time, like Freeman doesn't have enough to think about.

There are everyday occurrences that you and I take for granted, the sudden backfire of an automobile outside, watching television and seeing pictures of Cambodia, of Desert Storm, watching "Platoon."

He had to see the movie. I asked him over and over again, "Baby, are you sure that you can handle it?"

Abruptly, "Yeah."

He flipped. For three days he was gone, for three nights I couldn't sleep.

Between all the spurts of his street walking and all

the times of his pain, he continued to tell me about Vietnam. Having held it all inside of himself for over twenty years, his talking to me about it was like a giant abscess breaking. All the poison and noisome fluids came oozing out. I spent hours with him as he recounted the horrors to me, I began to smell, taste, and see what he was telling me as he went on and on about the carnage and death, over and over and over.

His night walking became more frequent as the emptiness that he was creating inside of himself began to fill up with an overwhelming guilt, guilt that he had made it back to the World, and that all of his buddies were left behind, their blood soaked into the jungle floors of Vietnam.

I know Doc as though he were alive. I know Freeman's pain so intensely that it has become my own. When he suffers, I suffer. PTSD, battle fatigue, shell shocked, whatever you call it, affects not only Freeman but me as well. We are both products of Vietnam.

Then, watching "Prime Time Live" and seeing the treatment the veterans are receiving for their wounds and afflictions, in payment for their willingness to lay their lives down for their country, at the VA hospitals across the United States. What gratitude!

People say, "Take him to the VA, he needs help."

I wouldn't take a dying dog there, I would take Freeman to my cat's veterinarian before I'd take him to the VA. He'd damn sure be better off... at least he'd be able to walk out of there on his own.

Doc, Wilcox, Gonzales, and Sonny have been showing up, uninvited. They are beckoning, saying the old infantry slogan, "Follow me." They are miniature replicas of themselves; they have their jungle dirty fatigues on, their steel pots, they are all cradling their weapons, M-16's and M-60's, across their laps. They sit there on my couch and hold a pipe up to him as an offering. They keep saying "Hey, L.T., come on, man." They beckon.

Doc, Gonzales, and Sonny died in Vietnam; Wilcox "followed them" when he bit the bullet back here in the World.

No one is equipped to deal with PTSD. I'm learning to, but have been afflicted with the disease myself.

He's the sweetest man in the world, but I'm the only one who knows it. I remember many things that have occurred over the years. The first real display of his heroism I can recall is when he saw a mentally retarded man being pushed around by four street people. They were using him like a pinball, they were the posts and he kept bobbing and weaving between them, he was whimpering every time they'd score a point. Freeman saw this and he flipped. His anger was immediate and consequential to the four slugs who all ran away, bleeding.

I remember another time when he was heading up to his favorite bar on Broadway; at the intersection of Broadway and Belmont an elderly woman had been struck by a car, she was lying in the middle of the street, conscious but obviously broken. Freeman ran out into the street, removed his jacket, and gently placed it under the woman's bleeding head. He stood up and gave the drivers in the cars the same look the Enemy had seen before he pulled the trigger or used his ranger knife to disembowel them.

Other pedestrians stood and watched. Freeman bent down on one knee, grabbed the woman's hand and murmured words of comfort. He looked up at the gathering crowd and said, "One of you motherfuckers go call a fucking ambulance NOW! Move, goddamn it, move!"

Back in '85, a wonderful man who I work with, Scotty MacGregor, had introduced my husband to a gentleman he knew who was the president of a factory on Chicago's Goose Island. I remember the look in Freeman's eyes when he received the call that he had gotten the job, so full of joy that it constricted my heart.

Those six months in 1985, before he got laid off with 85 percent of the other men at the factory, were the happiest six months of our lives together. For the first time in my life I didn't listen to what people had to say, most of the women I knew and worked with had said to me when Freeman started working, "He's going to leave you now, he doesn't need you anymore." I turned to them and replied, "Well, I guess we'll just have to wait and see, won't we?"

When Freeman got his first paycheck, he cashed it

and handed me the money, saying, "Sam, go down to Carson's or Marshall Field's on your lunch hour and buy yourself something pretty, like a nice dress or something. Get yourself some shoes to match and a purse too, and some of those other things that you womenfolk like to wear underneath, you know, something sexy." With his next paycheck, he sent me down there again. Then he started signing them over to me so I could put them in the bank.

I'd make him a lunch every evening that he could take with him to work the next day. He didn't miss one day in six months.

I was going through some personal changes myself during those happy six. I had received word from my physician that my Pap smear had come back showing pre-cancerous cells; I was inwardly devastated, since my mother had died of the same thing. I tried to keep my fear from Freeman, I didn't want him to worry about me. He offered to stay home with me when I went down to have the biopsy done, but I told him to go to work.

When it was over, after the doctor had cut five chunks of my cervix out to send to the lab, I walked the half block home and lay down on the couch. I remember the evening well, Freeman was working the night shift. The phone rang, it was Freeman on his lunch break. "Sam, how are you doin'?"

"I'm fine, Jeremy."

"What did the doctor say?"

I didn't pull any punches, "If it's pre-cancerous I'll just have to get a liquid nitrogen treatment, but if it's cancerous she'll want to put me in the hospital for laser surgery."

I could hear him begin to hyperventilate. "Jeremy, stop it!"

"Do you want me to come home, Sam?" His voice was full of fear.

"No, I'm all right, I'll see you when you get home."

"I love you, Sam."

"I know, Jeremy, I love you too."

"Bye, Sam, see you later."

"Bye, Jeremy."

I lay there and the monsters came back with their ugly faces, I fought them myself and tried to make them go away. It was the longest two weeks of my life, waiting for the results of the biopsy. When it came back, thankfully, it was the lesser of the two evils. Everything was going to be okay.

At Christmas time that year we had great fun shopping for each other. For the first time since we had been together, there were packages we had bought for each other wrapped up under our little plastic Christmas tree. We were like two little kids waiting impatiently for the day to come, and like two little kids we couldn't wait for Christmas, so we opened them up a week before.

There's a very violent side to my hero when he's provoked, but there's also a very warm, considerate, loving, and gentle side to him as well. It would be best when you see him sitting there in the dark corner of a bar that you leave him alone, he's most likely deep inside of himself and just wants to be. When he's open, laughing and joking with his buddies, it's safe to approach him... Just always remember what the government trained him to be if you decide to get in his face. Don't make his eyes change.

*I*t's nighttime again...

Freeman is in our bed lying next to me. I can feel his dreams, in my subconscious I know, although I am in a deep, dreamless sleep myself. I never remember the next morning waking him up, but he tells me and insists that I did. His inner self is calling out to me, the only person he ever trusted enough to call out to, "Wake me up!"

He's in the jungle again, a gook pursuing him, and all the men in his squad are gone, dead. I wake him up always just in the nick of time, the gook standing poised over him ready to shove his bayoneted weapon into Freeman's belly.

Time for more to die...

He sits on the edge of our bed with a very humiliated and defeated posture. The dream isn't fading, it's
growing in intensity. Is he awake? Yes. But he's back in
the jungle, back in our bed back in the jungle. The
dream won't let him go.

Jungle leaves are dripping...

He gets up and paces the floor, trying to walk off the
insanity, trying to get back to the World, to reality. The
bedroom walls start closing in, making him feel like being
buried alive. The linen on our bed becomes the lining of
his coffin, he feels as though he can't lie down there or
he'll die. He goes out of the room.

Monsoon water and blood...

The fiery ember of his cigarette glows and lights up
his face and the living room as I come around the corner.
I make obvious noises so he'll hear my approach. I clear
my throat of nothing, stamp my feet doing an insane
nighttime dance, and kick the bedroom door and curse
pretending to stub my toe.

The rain on the picture window is running and
dancing from side to side, mimicking his nighttime confusion. I sit down on the love seat next to his chair, letting
him know that he's not alone.

How's it feel GI...

The pain he feels is heavy, he's Atlas with the world

resting on his strong shoulders, his back straining and corded muscles popping out with his burden, getting ready to explode. "Why am I here and all my buddies dead?" He wonders about God, is there really such a being, and what kind of punishment will He mete out to him next? To us. I take the burden off his back as he begins to talk to me and I listen. I take his sins on as my own because he is willing to die for me, for my country.

To be this far away from home...

Monsoon rains are pounding the jungle leaves and the camouflage ponchos are dripping. Stereo sounds resound against the steel pot helmets, creating a jungle symphony. The darkness is ebony and hollow, fear is swimming in its cesspool and tunnel passage to hell. The picture window is a theater screen running the old movies of his memory. He sees only blackness, redness, bright hot white tracers from enemy fire.

Home where they call you names...

He reaches out for me and asks me the question over and over again, "Why did Doc die?"

I don't have an answer for him.

"Sam, maybe you should get somebody other than me. A guy that can really do things for you, things you deserve."

"I have what I want, Jeremy."

"Yeah, what? A fucked up Vietnam veteran? A

fucking baby killer?"

"It wasn't your fault," I say.

"Yeah, right. Why don't you get yourself a nice little white boy who can give you a little house with the white picket fence and 2.4 kids?"

"I have what I want, Jeremy."

And won't let you in the white man's door...

"Yeah, right. I can't even buy you things when I see something you would like up on Broadway. Do you know how that makes me feel?"

How's it feel, blood, laying here waiting to die...

He gets up and gets dressed. Nightwalker. I don't have the answers he wants, he thinks the bottle will. It's 2:00 am and he knows the bars that will still be open. I have to go to work soon, my eyes are exhausted from my tears after he walks out of the door. I lie there in the bed swooning with fear. I feel a great welling self-pity and think that maybe what he said to me before is true. Shame erases this thought as I lie there waiting to hear a car turn into the drive in front of our building and the automatic garage door click and whine upwards on its chain. It doesn't come and at 6:00 the alarm rings. God, I don't want to go, I don't want to leave him alone. I decide to call in sick and be here for him when he comes home.

For a country that doesn't even want you...

The answer's not in the bottle for that particular fact, either. If it was, the liquor companies would soon be out of business. The first time you popped a top the answer would come pouring out and you wouldn't need the stuff anymore.

I hear the rattle of his key in the door and it's a welcome sound. It's the same every time. He's angry because he finds me home, but his joy at having me there is evident to me in his eyes. He can't hide his feelings from me any more, like he used to be able to do when he first met me and I was very young. His manner is abrupt and hostile, but his eyes tell me something different.

When you make it back, black man, try to find a job...

The overwhelming guilt I feel because of my neglect of my good fortune. I have a job and I should be there today. He sits in his chair when I am at my job, looking at video tapes from movies he had taped the night before. Our apartment is filled with amusing diversions, two bookcases full of books, magazines from subscriptions I ordered for him to read, the VCR that fills his day with something other than his thoughts.

He's long since given up with the filling out of applications. When he walks into the room for the job he saw advertised and sees the other applicants sitting there, at least one hundred men in all, he turns around and walks out of the door he just entered. He's been offered different things... shady things. A man who had a plushcarpeted, paneled office in a stately Chicago hotel offered him a job. He looked at Freeman's military record and was very impressed at Freeman's qualifications. He was particularly interested in "sharpshooter." Freeman wouldn't take the job. Cash under the table, a lot of cash.

He had a job back in the seventies, a job that he had religiously gone to for five years. He was working for a company, operating heavy machinery and punch presses on an assembly line, and the supervisor in his department had announced that he was going to retire. Freeman knew, and so did everyone else, that he was next in line for the position. However, another man was brought in and Freeman was given instructions to train the man, a white man.

You'll sit there day after day looking at the sky...

At least the view is magnificent, with the Sears Tower visible on clear days. The building management washes the windows quarterly and for a week or so the view is sharp and hurts the eyes. Other buildings in the concrete jungle have smoke coming out of chimneys sticking out of their roof tops. The weather changing and bringing in storm clouds from the south can be seen rolling in to blanket the City. Old people walk with their canes as third legs along the sidewalk, making their way to the corner grocery store or to the restaurant where they hang out with their fellow retirees. Women clad in underwear twitch seductively down towards the rocks in the summertime. In the winter, the obese snowflakes from the lake area dance in front of the window, an annual burlesque.

What do you see, black man...

Sometimes he sees straight through the glass and past the horizon. Sometimes the glass becomes an opaque and milky-white theater screen.

Clouds dripping napalm, sun reflecting off dead men's eyes...

When I'm home with him and see him like that, I know. We have a little joke between us. I become the command post and call him back in from out in the field where he's doing his LRP.

"This is the rear echelon calling, this is the rear echelon, come in Freeman."

His head jerks toward me. "Sorry."

"It's okay now, baby," I try to tell him.

He grunts. He's trying to put the ruck down but the straps are melded into his shoulders and are attached under his skin. It won't come off, if he tries to pull it off his arms will come off too.

What do you smell, black man...

His whole being is immersed in his agony. His eyes cloud over again and I let him stay out in the jungle for a little while so he can relive his nightmare once more. He'll start talking to me soon, when he feels as though he's done his time in combat and is back in the bunker with his buddy Sam.

Mortar rounds, blood, and rotting bodies...

When you make it back, black man, you won't make it here...

We hold these truths to be self-evident.

You should have died for your country...

He couldn't agree with you more.

Been a good "boy" and died...

He almost did. He tried harder to do that too. He still has the pain and will always have the pain, burning, aching, constant, "hey you're alive boy," pain.

Your country doesn't want you, you don't fit in...

We hold these truths to be self-evident.

You never did, you never will.

He'll never stop having the dreams...

What can he say, he can't say nothing. If he started talking to you, you wouldn't believe or want to listen to him anyway. So, what's the use? He sits there with his half-hooded eyes looking out of the window at nothing. He sees nothing because he can't see past his pain, his pain that you would never understand, his memories of yesteryear, twenty motherfucking yesteryears ago, cloud his vision of everything you think you see plainly.

"Welcome home, GI. How's it feel after twenty years, us being so gracious to welcome you home with open arms? You ungrateful son of a bitch, you just sit there and don't even say thank you for the nice gestures we're extending to you."

216

Vietnam veterans had to wait for their ticker-tape parade, the ticker-tape parade they had to organize for themselves, the ticker-tape parade you should have given them a long time ago.

I remember begging him and pleading with him to go. He'd offer me no explanation besides, "The mother-fuckers can kiss my black ass." I could envision him there in my fantasies, dreaming while I was wide awake, seeing him march down the middle of the street with the others. I would be standing there clapping with tears running down my face.

The buildup to the big day received a lot of television coverage — what dignitaries are going to be there, how this is going to be the biggest and best parade ever. My Jeremy wouldn't go. On the day of the parade, I went to work and made a banner for him from a DrawPerfect program in the computer; if he wouldn't go to the parade at least I would welcome him home privately that night.

He got up that morning when I did and got dressed, he made no pretense that he would stay home that day. I asked him hopefully, "Jeremy, are you going to the parade?"

"Fuck no." He turned and walked out of the door without kissing me goodbye.

Freeman headed up on Broadway, to one of his favorite bars where he could sit and be left alone with his thoughts.

Later, when Jeremy sobered up I asked him to tell me the real reason why he didn't go to the parade. He was afraid. Ain't that a bitch? Do you want to know what he was afraid of? He was afraid of the names that you would call him again, "baby killer, monster, murderer."

Then I told him what it was like... I told him that when I was standing there at the corner of LaSalle Street and Wacker Drive clapping my goddamn hands off, that there was a lot of love in the air. There was no name calling, no ridicule, no derision, no malice, no contempt. No shouting "baby killer, monster, murderer."

It was just my luck, standing there when the Illinois veterans were coming around the bend. Jeremy should have been there, that was all I could think. I would have run right out into the middle of the street and planted a big, wet kiss right smack on his lips. Picture that, a woman crying with joy and looking quite crazy running out into the middle of the street and planting a kiss right flush on her veteran's jaw. Pretty picture, right? Just like the women did in celebration of the end of WWII. But Jeremy wasn't there.

I had stood there and applauded and lauded until I couldn't take it anymore. I had stood there and fantasized that Jeremy was in the parade. I wiped my eyes, and went back to my job. Another goddamn lie.

If he could go back he would, he thinks. If someone would offer him a job he'd take it. Mercenary work would be right up his alley. He knows what he does best.

He remembers and all he sees is the pain outside that window, the pain that is invisible to everyone else's naked eye. Let's call it his very own private hell on earth, his own Gethsemane, remembering the blood and the bullet-riddled corpses, remembering the screams of agony and the twitches of the men as they lay there dying, and in their delirium screaming, "Momma please help me!"

Momma is thousands of miles away baby, you're gonna die so stop calling for your momma like some motherfucker. Medevac's coming, maybe momma heard you after all. Look up in the sky… it's a bird, it's a plane, it's another motherfucking casualty because Charlie just shot the chopper out of the goddamn sky.

Cry GI, you're going to die. Momma can't help you now sonny boy.

"Oh God!" they scream.

Don't cry to God either, He's farther away from this motherfucking place than your momma is, boy, so stop your goddamn crying and die like a man.

He was gung-ho to get Charlie. He lay there on the monsoon soaked jungle floor firing his M-16 into the dense foliage.

"Die you slant-eyed, rice-eating motherfuckers!"

He saw his buddies that he'd been eating, sleeping, shitting, and surviving with lying there right next to him. Their eyes are getting mighty heavy, like big glassy marbles just waiting to roll back into their heads. Their chests are heaving and they are lying there crying for their momma. Some aren't saying shit, they are too shocked to feel or think anything, or too dead.

Thanks for the parade...

Freeman always stays in the bunker, our apartment. It's a haven to him, the only safe place that he knows. He has a replica of a grenade and a .45 hanging on the wall, and a real eighteen-inch machete like he used to cut the jungle foliage with in Nam. This is his new bunker, and I am a prisoner there with him.

He suffers from fear of the marketplace, agoraphobia, and this is the only place he wants to stay. Except when Nam gets too heavy on him and he has to walk the streets carrying his ruck.

I suffer from PTSD, I know more about Nam and the atrocities than I should. We carry the burden together, we share the ruck. I have the ammo, he has the 60... I have the C-rats, he has the P-38... I have the chopper, he is the door gunner... I have the water, he has the purification tablets... I have the grenade, he pulls the pin... I have the entrenching tool, he fills the sandbags...

It was three days. He was gone. I knew that something was terribly wrong. Then he gave me the ruck to carry. He told me that Jackson, the same Jackson whom he saw at his reunion, bit the bullet. His wife found him with his brains blown out.

Freeman walked out of the door and left me alone to deal with it.

I knew right then that Mrs. Jackson had to bury Vietnam.

I wondered, when will I?